The Fencepost Chronicles

"Like all master magicians, [Kinsella] makes the audience believe. He makes us laugh."

CALGARY HERALD

"Earthy. Funny, wry and poignant, yes, but decidedly earthy."

CANADIAN PRESS

"The book is a delight to read."

REGINA LEADER POST

Other Books by W.P. Kinsella

THE FENCEPOST CHRONICLES

WP

KINSELLA

The Fencepost Chronicles

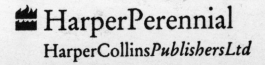

HarperPerennial

HarperCollins*Publishers*Ltd

First published by Collins Publishers: 1986
Sixth Printing: 1992

Canadian Cataloguing in Publication Data

Kinsella, W.P.
   The Fencepost chronicles

ISBN 0-00-647045-9

I. Title.

PS8571.I57F4 1990   C813'.54   C91-093076-7
PR9199.3.K59F4 1990

---

92 93 94 95 96 97 98 99 ALGER 15 14 13 12 11 10 9 8 7 6

CONTENTS

To my grandson Jason

The
Fencepost
Chronicles

TRUTH

No matter what they say it wasn't us that started the riot at St. Edouard Hockey Arena. The story made quite a few newspapers and even got on the Edmonton television, the camera showing how chairs been ripped out of the stands and thrown onto the ice. There was also a worried-looking RCMP saying something about public safety, and how they had to take some of the 25 arrested people all the way to St. Paul to store them in jail. Then the station manager read an editorial about violence in amateur hockey. None of them come right out and say us Indians was to blame for the riot; they just present what they think are the facts and leave people to make their own minds up. How many do you think decide the white men was at fault?

There was also a rumor that the town of St. Edouard was going to sue the town of Hobbema for the damages to the arena. But nothing ever come of that.

Another story have that the trouble come about because my friend Frank Fencepost own a dog named Guy Lafleur. Not true either. Frank do own a dog named Guy Lafleur, a yellow and white mostly-collie with a question mark for a tail. And Guy Lafleur the dog *was* sitting on a seat right behind our team players' box. That dog he bark whenever our team,

1

the Hobbema Wagonburners, get the puck. And every time he bark Frank would shout the same thing, "Shut up, Guy Lafleur you son of a bitch." A lot of heads would turn every time he said it, because, as you maybe guessed, St. Edouard was a French Canadian town. But it was something else that started the riot.

We never would of been there anyway if Frank hadn't learned to read and write. Someday, I'm going to write a story about the time Frank go to an adult literacy class. Now, just to show off, he read everything in the *Wetaskiwin Times* every week, even the ads. One day he seen a notice about a small town hockey tournament that offer a $1000 first prize.

"I think we should enter a team, Silas," he say to me.

"What do we know about hockey?" I say back. Neither me nor Frank skate. I played a little shinney when I was a kid, but I don't much like ice and snow up my nose, or for that matter, hockey sticks.

"Let's go see Jasper Deer," say Frank, "there's a $200 entry fee to be raised."

Jasper is employed by Sports Canada. All the strings on Sports Canada are pulled from Ottawa. Jasper he have an office with a gray desk big as a whale, in the Consolidated School building. About fifteen years ago Jasper was a good hockey player. I'm not sure what Sports Canada is, but I know they figure if they give all us Indians enough hockey sticks, basketballs and volleyballs, we forget our land claims, quit drinking too much, get good jobs so we can have the weekends off to play games.

Jasper is glad to have anybody come to see him. He was Chief Tom's friend, was how he come to get this cushy job, though he would rather be trapping, or cutting brush than sit in an office. He is already blearyeyed at ten o'clock in the morning.

2

"You want to enter a team in a tournament, eh?" he say to us, pushing his desk drawer shut with his knee, the bottles rattling.

Hobbema has a team in the Western Canada Junior Hockey League, so once guys turn 21 and don't get signed by any NHL team, they got no place to play.

"It'll be easy to get some good players together," Frank say, "and playing hockey keep us young people sober, honest and religious."

By the time we leave Jasper is anxious to put his head down have a little sleep on his desk, but he agree to pay for uniforms, loan us equipment, and rent us a school bus to travel in. I write down all those promises and get him to sign them.

Trouble is, even though a thousand dollars sound like a lot of money to me and Frank, the guys we approach to play for us point out it don't even come to $100 each for a decent sized team. So the players we end up with is the guys who sit in the Alice Hotel bar bragging how they turned down NHL contracts ten years ago, plus a few of our friends who can stand up on skates, and a goalie who just got new glasses last week.

The uniforms are white as bathroom tile, with a bright red burning wagon on the front, with HOBBEMA in red letters on the back. Some people complain the team name is bad for our Indian image, but they just ain't got no sense of humor.

Frank is team manager. I am his assistant. Mad Etta, our 400 lb. medicine lady is doctor and trainer, and Guy Lafleur is our mascot.

St. Edouard is way up in north-east Alberta, a place most of us never been before. Gorman Carry-the-kettle drive the bus for us. We have a pretty rowdy trip once we get Etta all attended to. She squeeze sideways down the aisle and sit on the whole back seat.

3

"I'm surprised the bus didn't tip up with its front wheels about three feet off the ground," say Gorman.

"Don't worry, you'll balance things out," we tell Gorman. He is about 280 lbs. himself, wear a red cap with a yellow unicorn horn growing out of the crown.

We stop for lunch in a town called Elk Point, actually we stop at the bar, and since most of the team is serious drinkers, it is 3:00 p.m. before we get on the road again. I have to drive because Gorman is a little worse for wear. When we get to St. Edouard, a town that have only about ten houses and a little frame hotel gathered around a wine-colored elevator as if they was bowing down to it, we find we already an hour late for our first game. They was just about to forfeit us.

The game played in a hoop-roofed building what is a combination curling rink and hockey arena. It sit like a huge haystack out in a field half a mile from town. Being February it is already dark. All I can see in any direction is snow drifts, a little stubble, and lines of scratchy-looking trees wherever there's a road allowance. The countryside is not too different from Hobbema.

Soon as our team start to warm up, everybody, except maybe Frank, can see we is outclassed. We playing the St. Edouard Bashers. Their players all look as if they drove down on their combines. And they each look like they could lift a combine out of a ditch if it was to get stuck. Most of our players are hung over. And though most of them used to be hockey players, it easy to tell they ain't been on skates for years.

The St. Edouard Bashers is young, fast and tough. Someone mention that they ain't lost a tournament game in two years. There must be 4,000 people in the arena, and they all go "Booooo," when our team show itself.

"I wonder where they all come from," says Frank. "There

4

can't be more than fifty people in the town; sure must be some big families on these here farms."

They sing the national anthem in French, and after they done with that they sing the French national anthem. Then about a half a dozen priests, and what must be a bishop; he got a white robe and an embroidered quilt over his shoulder, come to center ice where they bless a box of pucks. The priests shake holy water in each goal crease. The players all cross themselves.

"We should of brought a thunder dancer with us," says Frank. "Make a note of that, Silas. We do it next time."

I don't bother to write it down. I'm already guessing there won't be a next time.

Right after the puck is dropped St. Edouard take hold of it, carry it right in on our goal. They shoot. Our goalie don't have any idea where the puck is; by pure luck it hit him on the chest and fall to the ice. The goalie, Ferd Tailfeathers, lose his balance fall forward on the puck.

About that time a half-ton St. Edouard defenceman land with a knee on Ferd's head, smash his mask, his face and his glasses about an inch deep into the ice.

Guy Lafleur stand up on his seat and bark like a fire alarm.

"Shut up Guy Lafleur you son of a bitch," says Frank. Then looking out at the rink where Ferd lay still as if he been dead for a week or so, he say, "That fat sucker probably broke his knee on Ferd's head."

But the St. Edouard defenceman already skating around like he scored a goal, his stick raised up in the air, his skates making slashing sounds.

It is Ferd Tailfeathers get carried from the ice.

"Who's buying the next round?" he ask the referee, as we haul him over the boards.

"They take their hockey pretty seriously up here, eh?" says Frank to a long-faced man sit next to Guy Lafleur. That man wear a Montreal Canadiens toque and sweater, and he have only four teeth in front, two top, two bottom, all stained yellow, and none quite matching. I notice now that almost everybody in the arena, from old people, like the guy next to Guy Lafleur, to tiny babies in arms, wear Montreal Canadiens sweaters. Somewhere there must be a store sell nothing but Montreal uniforms.

"You think this is serious," the old man say, "you ought to see a wedding in St. Edouard. The aisle of the Catholic Church is covered in artificial ice, at least in the summer, in winter it freeze up of its own accord. The priest wear goal pads and the groom is the defenceman," he go on in a heavy French accent.

"I didn't see no church," says Frank, "only big building I seen was the elevator."

"You seen the church," say the old man, "elevator got torn down years ago. You guys should stick around there supposed to be a wedding tomorrow. The bride and bridesmaids stickhandle down the aisle, careful not to be off-side at the blue line; they get three shots on goal to score on the priest. If they don't the wedding get put off for a week."

Another old man in a felt hat and cigarette-yellowed mustache speak up, "We had one priest was such a good goaltender there were no weddings in St. Edouard for over two years. Some of the waiting couples had two, three kids already – so the bishop come down from Edmonton and perform a group ceremony."

Knocking Ferd out of the game was a real unlucky thing for them to do. I'm sure they would of scored ten goals each period if they'd just been patient. In the dressing room we strip off Ferd's pads, look for somebody to take his place.

Frank tell first one and then another player to put on the equipment.

"Put them on yourself," they say to Frank, only not in such polite language.

"You're gonna have to go in goal," Frank say to me.

"Not me," I say. "I got some regard for my life."

"Put your goddamned dog in the goal," say the caretaker of the dressing room. We can hear the fans getting restless. They are chanting something sound like "Alley, alley, les Bashers," and stomping their feet until the whole building shake.

"You guys should go home now," the old caretaker say. "They just looking for a bad team to beat up on. The way you guys skate it will be like tossing raw meat to hungry dogs."

"I think he's right," I say. "Let's sneak out. We can fend off the fans with hockey sticks if we have to."

We are just about to do that when Frank get his idea.

"It's why I'm manager and you're not," Frank say modestly to me that night when we driving back toward Hobbema.

We hold up the game for another fifteen minutes while we try to find skates big enough to fit Mad Etta.

Etta been sitting in the corner of the dressing room having a beer. Her and Frank do some fast bargaining. End up Frank have to promise her $900 of the thousand dollar prize money before she'll agree to play. Frank he plunk a mask on Etta's face right then and there.

"Not bad," say Etta, stare into a mirror. The mask is mean looking, with a red diamond drawed around each eye and red shark teeth where the mouth should be.

When we ask the Bashers to loan us a pair of BIG skates, they tell us to get lost.

"We've got to default the game then," we tell them, "guess

7

you'll have to refund all those fans their money."

That make them nicer to know.

"Yeah, we didn't bring them all the way up here not to get in a few good licks."

"Besides the fans are in a mean mood. They want to see some blood. We're going to get even for what happened to Custer," say their biggest defenceman, who is about the size of a jeep and almost as smart. He give us his extra skates for Etta, then say, "We'll score four or five goals, then we'll trash you guys for a full hour. Get ready to bleed a lot."

We set Etta on a bench with her back to the wall. Me and Frank get one on each side of her and we push like we was trying to put a skate on a ten pound sack of sugar.

"I'm too old for this," puffs Etta. "What is it I'm supposed to do again anyway?"

"Just think how you'll spend the $900," says Frank, tie her laces in a big knot, "and everything else will take care of itself."

Three of us have to walk beside, behind, and in front, in order to steer Etta from the bench to the goal. The fans are all going "Oooh," and "Ahhhh."

I get to walk behind.

"If she falls back I'm a goner," I say.

"So keep her on her feet," huffs Frank. "I figure you value your life more than most, that's why I put you back there."

"That's one big mother of a goaltender," say one of the Bashers.

"More than you know," says Etta, but in Cree.

"Alley, alley, les Bashers," go the audience.

Once we get Etta to the net she grab onto the iron rail and stomp the ice, send chips flying in all directions, kick and kick until she get right down to the floorboards. Once she got footing she stand with an arm on each goal post, glare fierce from behind that mean mask what painted like a punk rock album cover.

Soon as the game start again the Bashers get the puck, pass it about three ways from Sunday, while our players busy falling down, skate right in on Mad Etta and shoot...and shoot...and shoot. Don't matter where they poke the puck, or how often, there is always some part of Mad Etta blocking the goal.

After maybe ten shots, a little player zoom in like a mosquito, fire point blank; the puck hit Etta's shoulder and go up in the crowd.

"That hurt," shout Etta, slap with her goal stick, knock that little player head over heels as he buzz by the net. She get a penalty for that. Goalies can't serve penalties, but someone else have to. The Bashers take about twenty more shots in the next two minutes.

"You're doin' great," Frank yell from the bench.

"How come our team never shoot the biscuit at their goal?" Etta call back.

"We're workin' on it," says Frank, "trust your manager."

Things don't improve though, so Etta just turn her back on the game, lean on the net and let the Bashers shoot at her backside. There is more Etta than there is goal; even some shots that miss the goal hit Etta. I think it is a law of physics that you can't add to something that is already full.

There is no score at the end of the first period. Trouble is Etta assume the game is only one period long.

"I got to stay out there how long?" she yell at Frank. "I already earn more than $900. That little black biscuit hurt like hell," she go on. "And how come none of you guys know how to play this game but me?"

The players is all glassy-eyed, gasp for air, nurse their bruises, cuts, and hangovers.

9

As we guide Etta out for the second period, Guy Lafleur go to barking like a fire siren again. He always hated Mad Etta ever since one day he nipped at her heels while she huffing up the hill from Hobbema General Store, and Etta punted him about forty yards deep into the mud and bullrushes of the slough at the foot of the hill.

When she hear the dog Etta spin around knock a couple of us to the ice, make Frank afraid for his life, and go "Bow-wow-wow," at Guy Lafleur, sound so much like a real dog that he jump off his seat and don't show his nose again until after the riot.

The way we dressed Etta for the game was to put the shoulder pads on, then her five-flour-sack dress, then tape one sweater to her chest and another to her back.

Soon as she get to the goal she have to guard for the second period, she don't even stomp the ice, just fumble in the pocket of her dress, take out a baggie with some greenish-looking sandy stuff in it, sprinkle that green stuff all across the goal line. Frank rush off the bench, fall twice on the way 'cause he wearing slippery-soled cowboy boots.

"What are you doin'?" he yell at Etta, who is waddling real slow, force each skate about an inch into the ice every step, and is heading for the face-off circle to the left of her goal.

"If I stay in front of that little closet I'm gonna be so bruised I'll look polka-dotted. I've had enough of this foolishness."

"But the goal," cries Frank.

"Hey, you manage the team. I'll do what I do best," and Etta give Frank a shove propel him on his belly all the way to the players' gate by our bench.

As the referee call the players to center ice, Etta sit down cross-legged in that face-off circle, light up a cigarette, blow smoke at the fans who stomping their feet.

The St. Edouard team steal the puck on the face-off, sweep right over the defence and fire at the empty goal. But the puck just zap off to the corner as if there was a real good goalie there. After about ten shots like that the Bashers get pretty mad and the fans even more so. It is like Etta bricked up the front of the goal with invisible bricks.

The St. Edouard Bashers gather around the referee and scream at him in both of Canada's official languages, and all of Canada's swear words.

The referee skate to the net, test with his hand, but there is nothing to block it. He stick one skate into the net. He throw the puck into the net. Then he borrow a stick from one of the Bashers and shoot the puck in, several times.

"Stop your bitchin' and play hockey," he say to the St. Edouard players.

"I bet I could sell that stuff to Peter Pocklington and the Edmonton Oilers for a million dollars an ounce," Frank hiss into my ear. "You're her assistant, Silas. What do you think the chances are of getting hold of a bag of that stuff?"

"It would only work when Etta stare at it the right way," I say.

"Hey, Edmonton Oilers could afford to buy Etta too. She's more valuable than Wayne Gretzky. And we'd be her agents..."

"Forget it," I say. "You can't buy medicine."

Les Bashers keep shooting at our goal all through the second period and into the third, with no better luck.

It a fact of hockey that no matter how bad a team you got you going to score a goal sooner or later. At about fifteen minutes into the third period, Rufus Firstrider, who skate mainly on his ankles, carry the puck over the St. Edouard blue line, try to pass to Gorman Carry-the-kettle, who been wheezing down the right wing.

The goalie see the pass coming up and move across the goal mouth to cover it, and there's a Mack truck of a defenceman ready to cream Gorman if the puck even gets close to him. But Rufus miss the pass entirely, fall down and accidentally hit the puck toward the net and score. That is all the goals there is: Hobbema Wagonburners 1, St. Edouard Bashers 0.

It was them and their fans what started the riot. We all headed for the dressing room, except for Frank, who jump into the stands looking for Guy Lafleur, and suffer a certain amount of damage as a result.

After the RCMP cooled everyone off and escorted us to our bus, Frank show up with a black eye and blood on his shirt, while Guy Lafleur have a notch out of one ear but a big mouthful of Basher hockey sweater to make up for it.

They got carpenters screwing the seats back in place and men busy resurfacing the ice. The Bashers decide to start the tournament over the next day, playing against teams they can beat. They agree to pay us $2500 to go home and never enter their tournament again.

And that's the truth.

THE TRUCK

"How old does a truck have to be before it's antique?" Frank ask me. We is sitting in the Alice Hotel Bar with our girl-friends: Sadie One-wound is mine, Connie Bigcharles is his.

"Ain't sure," I say. "Antiques is usually cracked, dusty, and scarce."

"You figure Louis' truck would be an antique?"

"It's cracked and dirty," says Connie, "and I ain't ever seen a truck that old that's still running."

"What year is it?" asks Sadie.

"Nobody's sure. I think it started out as a 1947 Ford, but I'm sure every part on it been replaced at least once, and not always with 1947 Ford parts. It had at least five engines that I know of, and we had to change the registration numbers a couple of times to keep the finance companies from carrying it off."

I remember once Louis' truck got stopped at a road block in Edmonton and a constable look over all the papers I hand out the window to him.

"The serial number and registration show this vehicle to be a 1976 Cadillac Coupe de Ville," say the constable, scratch his head, breathe licorice into the truck as he shine his flashlight in the eyes of the eight or so people who jammed in

13

the cab.

"Shhhhh," says Frank, "we done that as a surprise gift for Louis, and we haven't told him yet. Louis always wanted to own a Cadillac, but this was the only way he could ever afford one."

"You must have to pay a lot larger insurance premium," say the constable, stare again at our pink insurance card.

"Well sure," says Frank, "Cadillacs is a lot more expensive to insure."

When we explain that Louis who own the truck is blind, that constable's eyes get big.

"Don't worry, he hardly drives at all anymore since he turned eighty," we tell the constable.

"They're right," says Louis, who we even forgot was with us: my sister Delores sitting on his knee in her chicken-dancer costume, pretty well cover him up. "Used to be I could tell the make of a car by the smell of it," Louis go on, "but last week I smelled a Fargo and it turned out to be a Jeep."

"But it had a Fargo bumper," says Frank.

"Still no excuse," said Louis. "I'm just getting old."

Even the constable have to smile at that, and since the truck appear to have insurance, and I got a driver's license, he let us go.

"How come you're all of a sudden interested in antiques?" Connie ask Frank.

"Well, I hear on the radio that Smilin' Al's Toyota Truck Center and Amalgamated Recreational Vehicle Showplace, just off 104 St. on the Calgary Trail, in Edmonton, the Oil Capital of Canada, going to give away a brand new Toyota truck; going to give 100% trade-in to the owner of an antique vehicle of some kind...but I didn't get the rest of the details."

"There has to be some kind of catch," I say. "If there's one thing we've learned it's that businesses never give away anything for free unless they profit ten times over from it. Also, Indians never likely to get any of the free stuff."

"Let's check it out anyway," says Frank, and the girls agree.

We drive up to Smilin' Al's place the very next morning, about fifteen or so of us in Louis' truck. Mr. and Mrs. Blind Louis is in the cab with us, Mad Etta our medicine lady sit like a queen on her tree-trunk chair in the truck box. We all feel kind of like we know Smilin' Al Nesterenko 'cause we seen him on the TV so many times. Smilin' Al have thin blond hair on a big, square head. He wear shiny blue suits with the jackets open so his belly can escape. He come on the TV grinning out of the side of his face and carrying a sledgehammer. He always standing beside an old car or truck.

"Friends," he say, "Smilin' Al Nesterenko is going to break down prices again," and then he swing the sledgehammer, bash in the windows and lights of that car or truck.

At one time Smilin' Al played tackle for the Edmonton Eskimos football team.

"Some people will say I blocked one too many field goals with my head," Smilin' Al will say into the camera, "and that I'm about eight bricks short of a load. But if my prices are too low who's gonna benefit, me or you?" Then he whack that car some more, sometimes even throw bricks through the windshield.

They say Smilin' Al comes to work in a green-and-gold painted limousine, drove by a guy in a football uniform. I don't think he's near as dumb as he pretend to be.

I notice as I park that there's a bunch of what are called Classic cars and trucks on Smilin' Al's lot. Most them are real old vehicles, but they been restored until they look better than new. Their bright colors and shiny paint always make

15

my mouth water. I sure hope that someday I get to own one of them.

"We come to win the new truck," Frank announce to the salesman who asked if he can help us.

"Good luck," say the salesman, "so did all these other people. What kind of car did you bring?"

"We brought our truck," we say. "It a genuine 1947 Ford," and we point it out at the curb, where it sort of droop like a frost-bit cabbage leaf. Our poor old truck sure look sad beside all these Classic cars.

"Here's a card with all the rules," says the salesman. "You'll have to get in line clear around the block there, if you want a chance to win."

I read the card out loud to everybody. The whole thing is pretty complicated. In the showroom window is a bingo machine, and inside the machine the little ping-pong balls, instead of having bingo numbers printed on them, have the make and year of a car or truck range from 1920 to 1963. Every hour from 10 a.m. to 10 p.m. three of these old vehicles get to line-up in front of the showroom window, and if the machine cough up the right make and model why the winner get to trade for a brand new Toyota King-cab truck, got automatic transmission, and every other extra known to white man and Indian. The card say that truck worth over $16,000.

One catch is, they write down your license number and you can only go through the line-up three times, ever. It don't look to me like the odds of winning are very good. It take us all that day, and after we park in the line-up overnight, half the next before we get to the front.

While we waiting we dream a lot about winning.

"It be kind of sad to part with this old truck," says Sadie. "How many babies you reckon got their start in here?"

says Frank.

We all think about that for a while, and we all talk up some memories, especially about times we been to the Golden Grain Drive-In Theater up near Millet. Drive-In theater known as Foreskin Park. Bet half the babies on Hobbema Reserve got their start there.

"Let's see," Louis Coyote say to his wife, get a nice smile on his old face, "I think we started off Jimmy, and Muriel, and Boniface, and Champagne...right here on the front seat. Maybe even a couple of others...who knows?"

"We haven't got a kid named Champagne," says Mrs. Blind Louis. Her and him can never agree, not even on how many kids there are in Louis' family.

"Sure we have," says Louis. "She's the second youngest. I seen her around someplace today," and he turn his milky eyes over the car lot.

"That's Charlene," says Mrs. Blind Louis, real cross.

"Close enough," says Louis. "She should be called Champagne; she's light and bouncy, taste sweet, and make an old man feel good."

"Oh, you knew my name all along, didn't you, Daddy?" say the little girl Charlene, scramble over two or three people, sit on Louis' knee and hug his neck.

When we get to the front of the line we feel kind of out of place, all of us jammed in our old rickety truck while beside us is two restored and rebuilt cars, a 1950 Ford and a 1956 Lincoln. Both shine like stars on water, even their owners shine, wear silky jackets, like expensive ski clothes.

Frank and me go into the showroom to see how the numbers get picked.

There is a real pretty girl there: second runner-up for Miss Edmonton Eskimo, somebody say. She wear a bathing suit and a banner say MISS AMALGAMATED

RECREATIONAL VEHICLE. She take the ping-pong balls out of the back of the machine.

"Just like a chicken laying an egg," says Frank.

She hand them to the sales manager who hand them to Smilin' Al, who announce the year and make.

When Frank try to push behind the machine, Miss Amalgamated Recreational Vehicle say "Where do you think you're going?"

Frank grin in that way he have that usually charm white ladies pretty good. But Miss ARV give him a push, stomp his moccasin with the back end of her high-heel shoe.

"Don't worry, I still love you," Frank say as he limp away.

We don't win. Not then or the next time we go through the line-up. We all go home disappointed. After we think about it we decide to plan a little before we come back.

"We need an edge of some kind," says Frank.

We ain't in much of a hurry to try again 'cause we heard somebody say it liable to be months before a winning number come up. Even then Smilin' Al ain't gonna lose much. Most of those restored cars worth up to $10,000 dollars or more.

I can see where Smilin' Al might not want us to win. I also figured Frank would be that *edge* he was talking about, only trouble is Miss Amalgamated Recreational Vehicle don't like him. But we got one more chance, there's a guy on the reserve name of Phil Carry-the-kettle, that I don't think ever been turned down by a woman.

I think I understand how Frank attracts girls, even though he ain't good-looking, dressed fancy, or drive a big car. He does unexpected things; he have more nerve than any other five guys put together; girls go for men like that.

Phil Carry-the-kettle, I can only describe as dangerous-looking – he is tall and dress like a cowboy: tight denim clothes, leather boots, vest, belt and hat. He always look as if he might go wild at any time – and it is that sense of danger attracts girls.

Some guys is surprised when women chase after them, but Phil ain't. I asked him one time how he managed it, and this is what he said: "Women are easy to handle as dogs, just look 'em in the eye and let 'em know you like 'em. Find out what they want from you: every one of them wants something, maybe it's just to be treated nice, to have a door opened or have you light her cigarette, or she might want to hear 'I love you,' or that you're interested in staying around permanent, or some girls just want a stud. It don't take long to find out. Then you give 'em what they want. And as soon as they get comfortable you take it away from them – that make them appreciate you more." Phil laugh and smile his lopsided smile at me.

"I should teach in a college, huh? That's how you handle women, Silas. I don't mind givin' away my secret. You can even write it down if you want. Real men are *born* knowin' how. If you have to ask, doesn't matter what you hear it won't do you any good. Most men are too chicken to carry out the last step; they're the ones end up married with a trailer-house full of kids and a finance company breathin' on them."

I'm not sure Phil is all that happy; he have lots and lots of women, but.... Anyway we figure if any guy we know can get close to Miss Amalgamated Recreational Vehicle, it be Phil Carry-the-kettle.

In order to get Phil to even come up to Smilin' Al's Toyota Truck Center, we have to promise him a hand-tooled saddle he seen in the window of Western Outfitter's Store in Camrose.

"Hey," we tell him, "soon as we win the new truck we'll sell the spare tire, the radio and the tape-deck and give you the money to buy the saddle."

"I don't work for promises," Phil says. So we have to pay him in advance. He is the kind of guy who might not keep his end of the bargain and we couldn't do a thing about it. Even Frank been known to leave the room when Phil Carry-the-kettle get riled up.

It probably best if I don't tell about how we got the saddle. Frank have to have a certain number of stitches taken at the hospital in Red Deer after he do the acquiring. And we all look nervous for the next week or two every time we see an RCMP car.

Phil drive up to Edmonton in his red sports car, ride alone, while all the rest of us cram in Louis' truck. But just like we figure, he hit it right off with Miss ARV. He take her home the very first night, and every night for the next two weeks.

"About the second night I was there her boyfriend came by, looked like a model for men's sissy clothing. I knocked him down two flights of stairs and he ain't been back," Phil tell us.

Phil also make us buy gas for his car, loan him meal money, and dancing and drinking money.

"Goddamn," says Frank, "if she decide to go on the pill we gonna have to pay the prescription."

I don't argue that it ain't true. But a few days ago Phil come up to me smiling and picking his teeth with a flavored toothpick.

"The whole thing is rigged," Phil tells me. "You know that machine that spin all the balls, well it sorts them all too." He go on to say that Miss Amalgamated, her real name is Debbie-June, goes behind the machine before every draw-ing, and as Smilin' Al looks out the window and announces what cars are competing, she takes out the balls for each one. Smilin' Al figures to let the contest go on for two years before he let someone win, and then it will be a friend or a relative or someone with a classic car worth almost as much as the new truck. He also told Debbie-June the contest has increased his business 50% already and he's getting more popular every day.

"Which kind is Debbie-June?" I ask Phil.

"What?"

"What does she want from you?"

"Oh," and Phil smile as the light dawns, shows his big white teeth. "She want it all. She like to be treated nice, told 'I love you,' and that I'm her permanent man. She need a stud service too, real bad," and he laugh some more.

"You think you can get her to help us?"

"Do birds have feathers? Listen, I'm gonna disappear for a couple of days. The day I get back she'll set herself on fire if I was to ask."

Phil sure know what he's talking about. He make himself scarce, and as soon as he do Debbie-June start looking pale and acting nervous as a mink. About every ten minutes she ask one of us if we know what's become of Phil and when he coming back.

"He's probably gone rodeoing," we say, "maybe to Arizona," and as we watch Debbie-June get an expression on her face like she just sunk a fish-hook in her finger.

"What are you guys hanging around here all the time for?" one of the salesmen ask us. "When are you gonna put your truck through the line-up again?"

"We got our medicine woman working on it," we say. And we have. Just to keep Smilin' Al and his friends busy, we had Etta set up shop in the parking lot. She build a real campfire on the pavement, boil up roots, and leaves and stuff in a saucepan we bought her. We tell Etta she is just a decoy, but she say it won't do no harm to cook up a real spell. Etta really like the orange-plastic truck-box cover that go with the pickup; with it she won't have to ride out in the open air no more. Some TV station even take pictures of Etta casting a spell so her friends can win a new truck, and her photo appear on the front page of the *Edmonton Sun*.

Three days later Phil come swaggering into the showroom. As I watch Debbie-June it look like her blood expand, because she get pinker, prettier, and taller, all in about one minute, not to mention happier.

"I'll just tell her unless she does what I ask her, I'll be goin' away again tomorrow," Phil whisper to me. "Better go get your truck in line."

Frank and Mr. and Mrs. Blind Louis spend the night in the truck in the line-up. It is about noon the next day before they get to the front.

Sure enough Smilin' Al stare out the window and announce: "In five minutes we'll have the next drawing. The vehicles eligible are a 1956 Lincoln Continental, a 1932 Chevrolet Coupe, and a...1947 Ford Pickup truck."

While he was making the announcement Debbie-June was nowhere in sight. Then Al grab a handle on the machine and it spit out three ping-pong balls. Debbie-June appear, pick up the balls and hand them to Smilin' Al, who put them in the side pocket of his suit coat.

He take the balls out one at a time and read them.

"1939 Terraplane," he say. "1955 Chev Bel-Air. 1947 Ford Pickup truck."

There is a very long pause and then all hell break loose.

Smilin' Al ain't smilin' anymore. He fire Debbie-June right on the spot, then look around to see who else he can make suffer.

But the sales manager get him by the arm and pull him off to one side, all the time pointing at the radio man who doing a remote broadcast from the showroom, and talking a mile a minute.

Smilin' Al finally calm down. Frank and Mr. and Mrs. Blind Louis come inside and he shake their hands, while we all clap and cheer some.

"This ain't a Classic car; this is a classic piece of junk," Smilin' Al growl when he examine Louis' pickup.

"It still won the contest," we say.

"I admit we won't be able to resell it," says the sales manager, "we'll just haul it directly to the junkyard."

"I'm gonna put it on TV and smash it all to rat shit," says Smilin' Al.

"Still, it's good publicity," says the sales manager. "Here, get a picture of the old man and his driver," he say to a salesman who carrying a flash camera. "When you stop to think about it we couldn't have a better winner than a blind 83-year-old Indian. We killed off three minorities all at once, so to speak."

"Face the camera, Mr. Ki-o-tee," say the man with the camera.

"You think that thing can steal my soul?" Louis ask nobody in particular.

"You already sold yours when you bought your Skidoo," says Mrs. Blind Louis.

Boy, the new truck sure is fancy. It is a King-cab, have little seats behind the regular ones that pop down. "Bet we be able to cram over ten people in here," says Frank.

"And that's just in the front seat," says Connie.

There is soft, fuzzy seat covers of a purple color and them seats lean back far enough to almost make a bed. Late one evening last week, Frank and Connie sneaked out there and tried them out for comfort.

Smilin' Al sign the new truck over to Louis, and Louis make his X to give the old truck to Smilin' Al.

"We sure gonna miss Louis' old truck," I say. "We all growed up with it around. It was kind of like a grandfather to us."

"You want to trade back?" says Smilin' Al. "Even up."

We thank him a lot but don't take up his offer.

We get lots of pictures taken with us standing beside the truck, and a newspaper lady write down all our names, even Mad Etta's, who tell her real name: Mrs. Margueretta Black Horses.

Frank seat himself behind the wheel.

"I want to *drive*," he says.

"You got to wait for us," I'm saying, but Frank ain't listening very good. He revving up the engine and I can tell he want to do a wheelie.

I think what happen is Frank's foot slip off the brake at the same time he revving the engine, 'cause I get just a flash of the surprised look on his face as the truck take off like a rocket, shoot across the parking lot, the service road, and right onto Highway 2, the main road between Edmonton and Calgary. There is a big screech of brakes, a clash of metal, and a dull bang like a far off explosion, then a lot of rattling, pinging, and popping as pieces of metal scatter across the highway.

We all run out to the highway, and there is our brand new truck crushed right under the back wheels of an eighteen-wheeler. Our truck been drug about a hundred yards and has suffered a certain amount of damage. Bet the driver of the eighteen-wheeler sure wonder where Frank came from.

On the other side of all the mess Frank is sitting on the road, he has lost his cowboy hat, one boot is off, and he got a look on his face as if someone just asked him a question that was too hard for him.

Mad Etta feel him up and down but he ain't neither bleeding or broken.

"Put this here blanket around him and sit him in the tr..."

We all realize together that our new truck is nothing but scrap and the old one belong to Smilin Al...for the time being.

"For winners we sure ain't got much to show for it," says Etta.

For once in his life Frank don't have nothin' smart to say. Connie kiss his face a few times and walk with one arm around his waist. The foot without the boot gettin' pretty wet on the slushy pavement.

BEEF

Sometimes being cheated ain't as bad as it made out to be. Back over a hundred years ago when the Government take the prairies away from the Indians and give us back these little reservations, our Chief Three Eagles make his mark to an agreement that, to help us Indians become farmers, the Government going to give every family two to four cows depend on its size.

But Three Eagles wouldn't accept the gift. I seen picture of Three Eagles wearing a breastplate, decked out in buckskin, feathers, and beaded wampum. He have the proud face of a hunter and warrior, and he wasn't about to be a farmer.

"I am not a tree," is what Three Eagles said. "My people do not root themselves to the land; we are traveling people. Indians soar like the birds. Just as the white man is a pale ghost of the Indian, so cattle are weak ghosts of buffalo. Farms are prisons. You do not put an eagle in a square cage."

It lucky Three Eagles died young.

We didn't know any of this history until I read in a magazine about how some Blackfoot Indians down south of Calgary, just last year hit up the Government for the cattle they was supposed to have got in 1877. They got a priest to do the research that prove their Chief Crowfoot refused the cattle, but that the Indians was still entitled.

Biggest surprise though was that it being an election year, the Government coughed up, not cattle but money.

The magazine explain it this way. "Both sides agreed early on that it would be foolish for the government to drive that big a herd onto the reserve: sorting, distributing, branding and fencing would have been virtually impossible."

Instead, every person on the reserve got $25 in cash money, and another 1.6 million dollars went to the tribe's bank account.

I showed the article to Bedelia Coyote.

"If it happened to the Blackfoot, I bet it happen to us Cree, too," I say. "I sure wouldn't mind that $25."

"You think small," says Bedelia. "You should be looking at the 1.6 million. Oh, what I could do with that..."

Bedelia is one of a group of young people has started a Back To The Land Movement. They think they can go back in the hills, hunt, trap, and live off the land like the old time Indians did.

Myself, I'm kind of fond of electricity, cars and televisions. But if that's what they want to do...

Bedelia take the case to a priest of our own, Fr. Alphonse up at Blue Quills School. He head right off to Edmonton to check over papers at the Parliament building and Provincial Museum. Guess he's happy to have something to make him feel useful. He don't have much success turning Indians into Christians, and spend most of his time read books in his office and say mass for two or three old women in babushkas.

To shorten up the story, it turn out we got the same claim as the Blackfoot, only there more people on Hobbema Reserve, so we have more cattle and money due us.

I lose interest after a while, but Bedelia and Father Alphonse push right on, even get the story and their pictures in *Alberta Report* magazine one time.

It take two years but the Government offer up something called Treaty 11, which offer the Ermineskin Reserve 4,000 cows and 40 bulls.

"What about the money?" say Bedelia.

"That's just another part of the process," say Fr. Alphonse. "We formally refuse the cattle and ask for money instead. We have to put it all in writing and it will take another year or two to resolve. We'll ask for the value of the cattle, plus compound interest for the last hundred years..."

"I'd rather have the cattle," says my friend Frank Fencepost. "If the tribe got a million dollars, you figure Chief Tom and his friends gonna let us get our hands on any of it?"

Frank and his girlfriend Connie Bigcharles has joined this here Back To The Land Movement though I'm not sure why. Only tool Frank really capable with is a bottle opener. As for Connie, she like tight sweaters, white lipstick and her "Pow-wow Blaster" radio, that all silver, big as a suitcase and can shake leaves off trees when the volume is up. Connie ain't never farmed in her life. She don't even grow houseplants.

I never thought I'd say this, but I think maybe it was a mistake for Frank Fencepost to learn to read and write. Ever since he done that, it open up to him about a hundred more ways to get into trouble.

Frank has learned to read upside down, so just by standing across Fr. Alphonse's desk he can read the name and address of the bureaucrat in Ottawa that the Ermineskin Nation Back to the Land Movement deals with.

Frank he grin like a Japanese general while he write to the Government say we happy to accept their offer of cattle and could they ship 400 a month until we get all of them. And he sign the letter Fr. Alphonse Fencepost, Instrument of God.

"*Fr.* could stand for Frank, couldn't it," say Frank. I suggest he send it to the Department of Graft, Patronage and Corruption, but Frank copy out the real return address from the envelope.

"Don't mess with your spiritual adviser," he tell me.

The Government write direct to Frank agree to send us the stock 400 at a time. And it coming in the name of the Ermineskin Nation Back to the Land Movement, Ms. Bedelia Coyote Executive Director. So there's no way Chief Tom can get his greedy hands on the cattle or the money they going to make for us.

"No problems," say Frank. "We just put the cattle to graze in the hills. The bulls make the cows pregnant. Our herd grows. We sell off the calves and yearlings – invest the money in real estate..."

"What about back to the land?"

"Hey, land is land. I'm gonna build my ranchhouse in Wetaskiwin; it have a three storey, twelve-suite apartment block attached to it."

But first we have to do a lot of work. We build a corral between Ben Stonebreaker's store and our row of cabins on the hill. We will put the first 400 cattle there, herd them in little groups to the pasture land. When we get the first 400 settled, we order 400 more.

The Bank of Montreal in Wetaskiwin after we show them the letter actually loan us some money to buy fence posts and log poles to make a corral. Out of that money Frank he buy himself a silk western shirt, cowboy boots, a ten-gallon white hat and a string tie.

"Just call me J. 'Tex' Fencepost," he says, and walk around with his chest pushed out, supervise the rest of us as we dig post holes and nail the poles into place with 6″ blue spikes.

Fr. Alphonse sure is surprised when he get a letter from the Department of Indian Affairs say they can't honor his refusal of the cattle because they is already on their way to us, and we should try to get our records in order.

Fr. Alphonse and Bedelia do a little investigating and discover what Frank has done.

"How could you do something so stupid?" roar Bedelia. Me and Rufus Firstrider is working on the corral. Frank laying down in the shade, his cowboy hat pulled down until his face don't show at all.

"Show a little respect for your ranch foreman," say Frank. "Besides, what's stupid? We got 400 cattle arriving, and they gonna come 400 a month almost forever. We get to keep the money we make. We all gonna be rich ranchers. Gonna call my spread the Ponderosa."

"We were going to do something positive," say Bedelia with less anger than I expected. "You'll be sorry," she predict before she stomp off.

As usual, Bedelia turn out to be right.

We actually get the corral finished the day before the first cattle due to arrive. I read somewhere about this here guy named Murphy who has a law about *Whatever can go wrong will go wrong*. I bet Murphy was an Ermineskin Indian.

Boy, we sure is excited when that first cattle transport turn off the highway and onto the main street of Hobbema. Little kids and old people are all along the street waving pennants left over from when the Edmonton Oilers won the Stanley Cup for hockey. People toot their car horns and wave.

The truck back up to the corral, let down its end gate and the first Herefords, with wine-colored bodies and square white faces step down onto the reserve. Eathen Firstrider, Ducky Cardinal, Gerard Many Hands High, and a couple of other guys who worked the rodeo circuit are there on their ponies to guide the cattle into the corral.

The second truck waiting to unload when the first one is empty. Then another one, and another, and another. Each truck hold about 35–40 cattle, and after a while it seem to me there is close to 400 cows in the corral. But when I look toward the highway there are cattle transports lined all the way down the hill and about four deep all along main street.

It seem some clerk in the Government in Ottawa add an extra zero to our order. And there is 4000 cattle arriving instead of 400.

"It ain't our problem," the truck drivers say. "Our orders are to deliver these cattle to Hobbema. This here is Hobbema. If you ain't got a corral, we'll just drop them in the street."

And they do.

By the end of that day there is more white-faced cattle on the Hobbema Reserve than there is Indians. The corral get so full it start to bulge at the seams. Then come a couple of trucks say they carrying the bulls.

"Can't turn these dudes loose," a truck driver say. "They're mean mothers if I ever seen some."

We have to chase a few hundred cattle out onto the street so the bulls can go into the corral.

"They must weigh 5000 lbs. each," says Frank, watching the wide, squat Hereford bulls wobble into the corral on their square, piano-legs. Each one got a bronze ring in his flat pink nose.

"Lookit the equipment on them suckers," says Frank. "I bet that's what I was in a former life."

"In the present one," says Connie, and Frank grin big.

The trucks just keep unloading. I guess word must work back to the end of the line that we ain't got no more corral space. Some of the trucks way out by the highway drop their loads and sneak away. Soon all the trucks are doing that. The main street of Hobbema look like a movie I seen once of a cattle drive somewhere in the Wild West of about a hundred years ago.

The cattle fill up the school grounds and is munching grass among tombstones in the graveyard behind the Catholic church. One step up on the porch of Ben Stonebreaker's Hobbema General Store bite into a gunnysack of chicken feed and scatter it all about. Four or five more climb onto the porch and one get about halfway into the store before Ben's granddaughter Caroline beat it across the nose with a yard stick and make it back up.

My girlfriend's brother David One-wound have himself a still in a poplar grove a few hundred yards back of town. RCMP can't sniff out his business, but it only take the cattle a few minutes to find it.

"They could work for the RCMP, use them as tracking cattle," says Frank. "And they'd be close to being as smart," he say.

The cattle like the sugar in the throwed out mash, and some of them get as close to mean as these docile kind of cattle can.

Ben Stonebreaker has five cattle prods in his hardware department, and he sell them out in about five minutes. Mad Etta our medicine lady was herding three or four half-drunk cows out of her yard when Ephrem Crookedneck, who decide to put as many cows as he can into his garden, what only fenced with chicken wire, and call them his own, either accidentally, or by mistake jab Mad Etta with his new electric cattle prod.

"Honest to God, I thought she was one of them. You seen her from behind. It was an honest mistake," he say, after the doctor taped up his cracked ribs and put his dislocated arm in a sling.

The cattle push up against the pumps at Fred Crier's Hobbema Texaco Garage, and before long one of the pumps leaning at a 45 degree angle. Old Peter Left Hand's chicken coop kind of sigh and fold up like a paper cut out, ruffled hens running everywhere, some squawking from inside the flattened building.

Traffic on Highway 2A is tied up, and somebody in a pickup truck hit a cow right in front of the Hobbema Pool Hall. Some young guys built a fire in a rusty oil drum and they barbecue the dead cow. Other guys is stripping down the pickup truck while the driver trying to call the RCMP.

"*We* is the law here," Rufus Firstrider tell the truck owner.

Constable Chretien and Constable Bobowski, the lady RCMP, come by, but there is some situations even too big for the RCMP. Constable Bobowski jump out of the patrol car, get shit on her boots, jump back in, then back out to wipe her feet on the grass. They stare through the windshield at the thousands of cattle milling around – some of them cattle bump pretty hard into the patrol car. Finally, they ease away a few feet at a time. I'm told they put detour signs on the highway a mile above and a mile before Hobbema.

It ain't near as much fun as we thought it would be to have 4000 cattle. Turns out nobody like our cattle very much. Cattle is dumb, and determined. They go just about anywhere they want to. They eat grass and gardens and leaves, knock down buildings, and some get in Melvin Dodging-horse's wheatfield, tramp down his crop. Six or seven of them eat until they die. Then they smell up the air on the whole reserve.

White farmers and even some Indians claim they going to sue the Ermineskin Nation Back to the Land Movement. The main street, and the gravel road to the highway, and even the walking paths is covered in cow shit. Seem like everyplace you can name is downwind of our herd.

It is also pretty hard to keep 40 bulls in a corral when there is close to 4000 cows outside the corral.

"Do something," everybody say to Bedelia Coyote and Fr. Alphonse. But there is a point where people get overwhelmed by a situation and Bedelia and Fr. Alphonse is in that position.

People try to get Chief Tom in on the act, but he stay in his apartment in Wetaskiwin with his girlfriend, Samantha Yellowknees, and after they put pressure on him, decide he have serious government business in California for the next month. Chief Tom don't like the smell of cattle no better than the rest of us.

Everybody grumble. But we got what we said we wanted. It pretty hard to complain about that.

Everybody now eat good anyway. Old hunters like William Irons and Dolphus Frying Pan, have a couple of cows skinned and quartered before you can say, "hunting season," and everybody got steak to fry and liver to cook. William and Dolphus have blood up to their elbows and they ain't smiled so broad since they got too old to go big game hunting.

Next morning a tall cowboy arrive with a cattle transport offer to buy up cows at $400 each. He put down the ramp at the rear of his truck and pay cash money to whoever load an animal up. He load up 40 cows and promise to come back as soon as he can.

"If he's paying $400, these here animals must be worth a lot more," says Frank.

All the time the truck was being loaded, Bedelia was yelling for them to stop, shouting about our heritage and don't sell the future for pocket money. But nobody pays any attention and somebody even shove her out of the way, hard.

Frank get Louis Coyote's pickup truck and using the same ramp we use to load Mad Etta when we want to take her someplace, we get three cows into the truck box rope them in pretty tight.

Frank he head for Weiller and Williams Stockyard in Edmonton.

Most of us don't really have any idea how much a cow is worth. But after Frank make that first trip to Edmonton he report, "They is paying 80¢ a pound and these cows weigh around 1000 to 1200 pounds." The three he crammed in Louis' pickup truck bring $2640 cash money.

When people find that out everybody want to get in on the act.

When the cattle transport come back, David One-wound announce we going to "nationalize" it and the driver just barely get away with his empty truck and ten guys yipping on his heels.

A couple of people load cows into their wagon boxes and start their teams out for the long trip to Edmonton.

Some of the young cowboys like Eathen Firstrider, Robert Coyote and Ducky Cardinal decide to do a real cattle drive and start about fifteen cows in the direction of Edmonton.

Some other people tie a rope to the neck of the tamest cow and lead her, walking in front of her, in the direction of Edmonton.

Bedelia is still yelling at people to stop and is still getting ignored. Fr. Alphonse gone back to his office at the Reserve School, wishing, I bet, that he'd never found out about us being cheated.

It is kind of sad to see all the crazy goings on. If we could just get organized we could make a lot of money for years and years to come. But people ain't ready to listen to Bedelia; they just go on their own way selling cattle here, there, and everywhere. Local white farmers stop people as they walk up the ditches offer less than half what the animal would bring in Edmonton. But people is too greedy to say no. Ogden Coyote trade a cow for a 10-speed bicycle, have bright pink tassels on the handlebars.

I remember reading in, I think it was *Time* magazine about how in Africa, when some little country that been a colony for a thousand years get its independence, the people don't know how to act. They spend foolishly, act like fools and their country end up in a terrible mess.

I wish I was a leader. I can see what should be done, but I don't know how to go about it. I'm a watcher.

"*You* could stop this foolishness," I say to Mad Etta. "People would listen to you. Why don't you do something?"

"Hey, they *are* doing what they want. Water rise to its own level. You put food in front of hungry people they going to eat good before they think about planting seeds for next year. Same with money. I know what should be done, but the people ain't ready for it yet. Maybe, Silas, when you're an old man..." and she stop and stare wistful off into the woods behind her cabin. "But in the meantime, I got a bull and six cows tethered in the pines down the hill. How soon you figure we can use Louis' truck to take them to Edmonton?"

The next morning Frank come bounding into my cabin, smiling like he just got it on with a movie star.

"Hey, Silas, our troubles are over," he yell. "I had me a dream last night and these here cattle going to make us rich."

"How are they gonna do that?"

"All we need is some old sheets and some paint."

"For what?"

"Hey, we gonna sell advertising space on our cattle." Frank is grinning so wide I'm afraid he's gonna dislocate his ears.

"That's crazy."

"No it's not," and Frank jump up on a kitchen chair, then jump off quick, run to my bed and pull a sheet off with one hard yank, leave the rest of the blankets and Sadie right where they were. He set two chairs about four feet apart and drape the sheet over the chair backs.

"Pretend that's a cow. We tie a sheet over her, then..." and he pull from his pocket a huge magic marker about the size of a shock absorber, and paint on the sheet HOBBEMA TEX-ACO GARAGE. "We do that on each side of the cow, then we put them to grazing along the highway. They'll be just like billboards."

No matter what I say to Frank, whether I laugh or make fun of his idea, he stick to his guns.

"There's only one thing to do," I say, "let's go make some sales calls."

In Wetaskiwin we get a parking place in front of Mr. Larry's Men's Wear, COUTURIER TO THE DISCRIMINATING GENTLEMAN.

We troop inside.

"We're here to see Mr. Larry," I say to a tall man dressed so fancy he could lay right down in a coffin and feel at home.

"I am Lawrence Oberholtzer, the proprietor."

"I'm Frank Fencepost, ace advertising salesman. How do you like me so far?" and Frank stick out his hand grab one of Mr. Larry's long pale hands that was by his side, and shake hearty.

"I would just as soon not answer that," he say, his voice able to freeze water or shrivel plants.

"I'm gonna show you how to become the richest busi-nessman in Wetaskiwin."

"I already *am* the richest man in Wetaskiwin," say Mr. Larry. "Now please get to the point."

"How would you like to have 4000 cattle with your name on them?"

"Don't tell me; you're cattle rustlers."

Frank explain his idea.

"You can even advertise on more than one cow. Show him, Silas. This is my assistant Silas Running-up-the-riverbank."

Mr. Larry nod at me.

"Picture your cows grazing in a row beside the highway, Mr. Larry."

I take out four sheets I been carrying, unfold them, drape them over racks of suits. When I finished they read like this:

> THIS HERE STORE
> IS A FANCY PLACE
>
> SHIRTS & SUITS
> FOR EVERY RACE
>
> CHINK OR JAP
> CHRISTIAN OR JEW
>
> MR. LARRY'S
> IS THE STORE FOR YOU.

Frank he look so self-satisfied he just know it is impossible for Mr. Larry to turn him down.

Out on the street we gather up the sheets from where Mr. Larry threw them and decide to call on Union Tractor Company.

Six businesses later, we put the sheets in the truck and head for the Alice Hotel to have a beer.

"They'll be sorry," says Frank. "I can't help it if I fifty years ahead of my time."

The cattle problem solve itself, sort of like flood water recede slow until you never know the water been high at all.

Everybody on the reserve eat good for a few weeks. The old

hunters is happy as pigs in a barnyard. A lot of us carry cattle off to sell in Edmonton. Louis Coyote buy twin Skidoos for him and Mrs. Blind Louis.

I buy me a new typewriter but it ain't no smarter than my old one, so it get pushed to the back of the kitchen table and my little sister Delores, who claim she going to tell stories just like me, pound on it once in a while.

Frank buy a video recorder and him and Connie pick out about a hundred movies. Frank is working on tapping into the power line to the UGG Elevator so's they can watch movies soon as they get a TV, which Frank is working on too.

Mad Etta was about the only smart one, she corral two of them Hereford bulls, and got them in separate pens behind her cabin. We drive her around to local farms and she sell their services.

"Etta ain't going to go hungry for awhile," she says, rocking back and forth on her tree-trunk chair. "It sure nice to be supported by somebody who enjoy their work," she say and laugh and laugh.

"It's back to the drawing board for us," say Bedelia and Fr. Alphonse. "We got a lot of work to do yet," they say. According to them, the Cattle Treaty was only one of 23 claims outstanding. They going after money for land of ours been given away, used for highways, irrigation canals, and Government Experimental Farms.

"Anytime you need help negotiating," says Frank, "the great Fencepost is available, free of charge."

Frank never quite understand why they don't answer him back.

THE MANAGERS

For Jim Jamieson

This time the trouble start when a black limousine with blue-tinted windows turn off the highway and pull up to the Hobbema General Store. The passenger window purr down and a tough-looking dude with more scars on his face than a nine-year-old's knees, call me over with a beefy finger.

"We're here to pay a call on the chief," he says.

"Yeah, well this is just the reserve, you won't find no chief here."

"Well, where will I find him?"

"Depend on what you looking for him for."

"What do you mean?"

"Well, he might be someplace if you was wanting to pay him money, while he might be someplace else altogether if you want to collect money from him."

"I understand *that*," say the guy, who wear a woolly-lamb of a hat that make him look like a Russian secret agent. "We have a business deal to discuss, guaranteed to make lots of money for your tribe."

"If this deal's so good," say my friend Frank Fencepost, who's wandered over, along with Eathen Firstrider, "How

40

come rich white guys like you want to share it with us poor Indians?"

"A matter of capitalization," he say, "you understand capitalization, Tonto?" And the guy curl up one lip to show a lot of white teeth.

It is a bad mistake to get on the wrong side of Frank Fencepost. Mad Etta is the only person it is worse to have for an enemy.

"I just learned to read and write," says Frank. "I put a capitalization at the beginning of each sentence, use one for names, places, proper nouns. Like if I say to you, 'Hey, Dirt Bag,' all three words would get capitalization." And Frank put one of his big hands on the window frame, stare in without blinking at the scar-faced man.

"Hey, no offence," says the guy, make a weak smile. "I could make it worth your while to find the chief."

"Chief lives up the hill there where there's no roads, but we could walk you up easy."

The guy lean across and talk to the driver who we ain't had a good look at yet. They both turn their necks around and we guess there must be somebody in the back of the car, too.

Nobody say anything but the three doors of the Cadillac open quiet as if they had no locks and three guys step out. They all wear dark topcoats. All three is short and broad, two have slick black sideburns, while the guy in the back have hair the color of white marble. All three look to be tan although it is barely June.

The three guys are named Gino, Rocco, and Mario.

"We're Hughie, Dewey, and Louie," says Frank, who got a box with about 5000 comics on the back porch of his cabin.

"Nice to meetcha," says Rocco, who is the one with the woolly-lamb hat.

Just before we walk these here parties up to the cabins,

41

Frank stick his head in the door of the pool hall and whistle up the David One-wound Auto Parts Co., who is my girl-friend's kid brother, and his friends Michael Bonneyville and Wilfred Robe. On days when there is nothing to do on the reserve, which is most of the time, they practice stripping down cars and putting them back together.

"Joy to watch," is how Ben Stonebreaker, of Hobbema General Store, describe what they do. "There should be an Olympic event for them to enter, 'cause I bet they is the best in the world."

The hill is steep, and the road greasy and muddy, and these dudes skid around pretty good in their slippery city shoes.

We take them to Mad Etta's cabin. Rufus run ahead so Etta is expecting us. Rufus let us in and he have the guys take off their hats and coats. Rufus set the men on two old kitchen chairs and a nail keg. We can hear Etta moving around behind the blanket partition, make puffing sounds, and other noises sound like she doing something rude to a piece of venison.

"I thought you said these Indians were rich?" say Gino, who is the older one.

Rocco just look uncomfortable and don't say nothing.

Etta waddle out from behind her sheet; she wear her five-flour-sack dress, got squirrel tails pinned down the sleeves and sides, got more elk teeth glued to her than you find in a medicine man's bottom drawer. The teeth shine like ivory in the lamplight.

Etta perch herself up on her tree-trunk chair where she look down on the three visitors.

"That will be $25 each, please," she say in a deep voice.

"What the hell for?" say Rocco.

"Old Indian custom," I say.

"Sort of a gesture of friendship," say Frank.

"You get it back if the deal go through," add Rufus.

Gino snap his fingers and Rocco dig in his inside pocket, take out a big, expensive leather wallet, and hand me $75, which I pass on to Etta.

"Now what is it you want?"

"Well, sir, we represent certain parties who have a very lucrative financial..."

"No. No. What's the matter with you?"

"The matter?"

"What sickness do you suffer from?"

"We ain't sick. We came to..."

"Don't waste your medicine man's time..."

"Aren't you the chief?"

"Chief!" I say in a surprised voice. "We thought you wanted the medicine man."

"We said chief," Rocco say real loud. "Where's the chief?"

"Oh, he live in Wetaskiwin. We take you right there. We sure sorry for the misunderstanding."

Rufus already handing them their coats and hats.

"How about our money?" says Rocco.

"Did the deal go through?" says Frank.

"Well, no, but..."

"No deal, no money, let's move right along," and we all file outside, leaving Etta, sitting in her chair, smiling up her sleeve where the $75 is sleeping.

When we get back down the hill, that big limousine suffered a certain amount of remodeling. It sitting on its rims with the hood and trunk both up and all the doors open. The radio and stereo and air conditioning is gone, along with the spare wheel, the front bumper and grill, and any engine parts that unscrew quickly.

"What's happened here?" say Rocco.

"Your car's been stripped. You never seen a stripped-down car?" says Frank, and grins big.

Rocco fumble in his inside pocket again, come out with a mean-looking gun so big it's a wonder it don't tip him over.

"You gonna put the car out of its misery?" say Frank.

"No, I'm gonna shove this up your nose and keep it there until the car is back together again." And he move toward Frank.

Frank duck around a kerosene barrel on the porch of the store. "Hey, it's a matter of capitalization, Rocco. You should understand that..."

Before Rocco can go on, Gino snaps his fingers again.

"It's a City car, for chrissakes," he say, "forget it. We want to see your chief and we'll pay you $25 each to take us there," he say to us.

"Why didn't you say so in the first place?" we say, and I run across the street start up Louis Coyote's pickup truck. Rufus take his $25, decide to use it to buy groceries. Gino sit in front with us, while we put Rocco and Mario in the truck box.

Everybody I know from our reserve is either real poor, plain poor, or just getting by. But that don't mean there ain't quite a bit of money around. Money that pass through the hands of us Indians, not me and my friends, but the bigshot Indians like Chief Tom and his cronies. "Pass through the hands," is how Indian Affairs people talk, when they speak to the newspaper or TV about a business venture that gone bad. And we had plenty of those.

Militant Indians yelp like hungry dogs but not much else. The ones who go along with the Establishment are the ones able to get their hands deepest into the government pockets. They first make the government people feel guilty about how us Indians been treated, then they propose a business deal; a landscaping company, a furniture-making company, a fish-packing plant, and the government put up half the money while the other half come from oil royalties held in trust for our tribe. That money come from the government, pass through Indian hands, and end up in white pockets.

Indians like Chief Tom and his friends fancy themselves businessmen, but as Mad Etta say, "It like dressing a coyote up in a suit and tie. Underneath his suit, he still a coyote. Only talent they have is for making white people feel guilty. They don't know nothing about managing money, not that they should, but they too proud to get smart businessmen to help them. Instead they take help from the first white people who offer it, which is the same people been selling Indians bad liquor, cheap clothes, junk food, and cars with bad transmissions for the last hundred years or so."

The landscaping business lost $300,000, and the furniture-making company turned out to be making furniture that was twenty years out of style: $500,000 lost. There ain't anywhere this side of British Columbia can produce enough fish to keep a fish-packing plant running, and even then the fish cost twice their worth to truck in: $1,000,000 down the drain.

Some smiling guys from Hollywood with about a million dollars worth of gold chains around their neck, sweet talk nine million dollars to make a movie about an Indian. They got a famous white actor to play the Indian, and the movie showed for about three days at theaters in Edmonton and then disappear into wherever those kind of movies go. I heard they were going to show it on TV in Italy. I guess they like Indians in Italy.

Chief Tom wearing more expensive suits these days and his girlfriend Samantha Yellowknees driving a white Porsche. Her and Chief Tom flew to Hollywood for thirty days to sign the movie contract.

Chief Tom live in a fancy apartment in Wetaskiwin, got a squawk box at the front door, a sauna bath and a swimming pool in the basement.

Samantha Yellowknees answers the door, and she, like always, wear a lemon-colored dress, make her look cool as a glass of Kool-aid. She have her hair up in a bun, and carry a clipboard.

Gino introduce himself, bow a tiny bit and kiss her hand.

"These here is Rocco and Mario," Frank say. "They're flunkies. Rocco's hobby is manslaughter," and Frank grin.

"My assistants," Gino say in a resonant voice like a priest.

Chief Tom is wearing a blue velvet smoking jacket. Their apartment got more furniture in it than a second hand store, and it even closer together. I think the Chief and Samantha must of gone through the Marv Hayden Furniture Store in Wetaskiwin and said, "We'll take one of each."

Rocco and Mario look a little worse for wear, there ain't much in the way of springs in Louis' truck and we didn't spare the bumps on the way to town.

"They're bouncing like rubber balls back there," Frank say at one point on the trip into town.

"It's good for them to be put in touch with their roots occasionally," said Gino, and he smiled by moving his upper lip up.

"Here's the deal, your highness," Gino say to Chief Tom, after we all get settled in the living room. When he hear those words the chief expand about an inch in all directions, and his mouth form a self-satisfied little smile, though it try not to.

"We are, ah, brothers representing a certain city in Montana. The city owns a baseball team, the Montana Magic of the Universal Baseball Association. The team has recently become available, and since your tribe is known to be interested in lucrative investment opportunities, we thought we'd take the liberty of making an approach, and since you yourself have a reputation as a shrewd businessman, we thought we'd come directly to you."

"If he butters him up anymore Chief Tom will squirt right across the room," whispers Frank.

If there's one thing Chief Tom understand it is flattery. I guess that because he's a politician. I remember Mad Etta saying, "To be a politician you got to know how to flatter and lie."

"The Montana Magic was purchased by the city in question about a year ago. The operation has been very successful, but the city doesn't feel it should be involved in private enterprise of this nature..."

Pretty soon Chief Tom get out a bottle of brandy and little pot-bellied glasses for everybody, even me and Frank.

At first Chief Tom try to get rid of us.

"Thank you, Simon," he say to me, "for delivering these gentlemen. You can run along now."

Frank already plopped down on the sofa and got his boots on a glass-topped coffee table.

"We'd sure like to stay, Chief Tom. We're studying this here business management course at the Tech School, and we'd like to see how a real professional businessman like you do things."

"Well," say Chief Tom, pointing at us but talking to Gino and his friends, "I always like to try to do everything possible to stimulate the intellects of our young people like Frank and Simon."

"By the way, my name's Silas."

"Whatever," say Chief Tom.

Gino go on to explain that there's a baseball park and land go with the team. "Very profitable," is how he describe the operation, again and again.

"What we had planned to do was drive you down to see a baseball game tomorrow night, but we had an unfortunate problem with our car out at the reserve..."

"Wasn't us," say Frank.

"Just send the bill to the Ermineskin Tribal Council," say Chief Tom.

"Very kind of you," say Gino. "But I think I have an even better idea. I'll charter an aircraft and fly you down tomorrow. At my expense, of course. How would you like that?"

Chief Tom expand about another inch and accept.

"And you young men are cordially invited," say Gino. "It will be a good lesson in business for you."

Boy, I never been in one of these private planes before. It seat eight people, got eight velvet seats and a bar and everything. There is Gino, me and Frank, Chief Tom and Samantha, and the pilot. Rocco and Mario get to stay behind and wait for the car to get fixed. I bet Chief Tom sure be surprised when the bill come to six thousand dollars or more for missing parts on that limousine.

"See, there it is, right down there," say Gino after he have the pilot fly right over the stadium.

That baseball park ain't exactly what we expected. It ain't in the city, but is a full two miles out of town, off a gravel road, sitting like a button on the prairies, what are wide and green for as far as one care to look.

The second time we ever seen the baseball field we was riding in the back of another limousine, and it dark, the way only the prairie can be at night. Gino stop that car, pull off the road a half mile or so from the ballpark, and we step out of the car. The air is dew-damp, and the only sound is a few insects ticking and purring. We're too far away to hear any sound from the stadium. The ballpark look like a splash of molten gold. My blood speed up, and every one of us breathe deep of the night air, what have a bite to it, even in June.

"I bet that's what the end of the rainbow look like,"

whisper Frank, who ain't one to be in awe of very many things.

Behind a green board fence is a small grandstand. Only way it is different from the seating along first and third base is that the bleacher is closed up so you can't toss garbage or see down to the ground. There is a tiny trailer behind the main grandstand that open up to be a concession. And there two trailers outside the outfield fence, one used as a dressing room, the other as an office and home for the managers of the team. Eight tall, silver light standards gleam down onto the field.

And boy when we get up close we see that baseball stadium, what have a name, Magic Field, is about as full of people as it can get. Gino has been saying it hold 4,000 people. "Of course," he say, "you won't expect it to be full tonight, after all this is only a Tuesday, the crowds don't really come until the weekend."

But it is full, and there three lines of people back half a block from the concession, and kids with baskets sell hot dogs, beer, peanuts, and ice cream all through the stands.

Samantha look at the ticket prices, ask again how many people the place hold, make a bunch of chicken scratchings on her clipboard.

"Fifteen thousand dollars," she whisper to Chief Tom.

"How many games do they play a season?" ask Samantha.

"Fifty games at home, fifty on the road," answer Gino.

"How do you get more people in here on the weekend?" ask the chief. "Looks to me to be full up tonight."

"Oh, well, we cheat a little," says Gino. "We sell Standing Room tickets and people stand along the foul lines, even sit against the outfield fence."

"Three quarters of a million dollars, not counting the concessions," Samantha say toward Chief Tom's ear, and the gold of the floodlights reflect in both their eyes.

The Montana Magic baseball team get beat pretty bad. In fact, except for about three players they look like some of the teams our Hobbema Buffaloes baseball team play against in the summer. I bet our pitcher Gorman Carry-the-kettle, could of done as good as the guy who pitch for the Magic.

"People come here to watch baseball," says Gino. "It doesn't matter whether the team wins or loses, although winning is better," and he smile real friendly. "But it's the game that counts, the thrill of competition. After all, this *is* America."

The Magic have orange and black uniforms, just like Hallowe'en costumes, and they play against a team from Carson City, Nevada, which I think is a long way away.

Gino get us all rooms at the Holiday Inn, tell us to charge our meals. Frank he get a date with one of the girls who sell hot dogs, keep her overnight with him. The next morning the three of us look around downtown while Gino take the chief and Samantha to "look over the financial end of the operation."

"Don't worry," Frank tell the girl who is named Cindy, or Cathy, or Candy, and is still wearing her orange and black concession uniform, "me and my friend here going to buy the team and we'll be here all summer to manage it." Then he phone room service and order up six cheeseburgers to go, in case we get hungry on the plane.

Gino see us right back to Chief Tom's apartment. He kiss Samantha's hand again, and shake hands all around. "We'll be waiting at the TraveLodge for your decision," he say.

"That sound like an interesting business proposition," the chief say to Samantha, as soon as Gino is gone. "The financial incentives look propitious. I think we should recommend accepting this financial equity, when the Band Council meets tomorrow."

Samantha just go, "Ummm," and scribble madly on her clipboard.

"Chief Tom," I say, "what I wonder is, if that team doing as good as they say, why do they come looking for investors? If it's so good, there should be a lineup of people waiting to invest."

But the chief he spout some more double talk and don't even come close to answering my question. I can tell by look at the set of his mouth that the Ermineskin Indians going to own themselves a baseball team.

That's when I start to think on what Frank told that girl as a "lover's lie." Soon as we're outside I say to Frank, "Hey, if the band buy that baseball team, they *are* going to need somebody to manage it."

"You figure you could do it?"

"Both of us," I say. "One of the things I've always wanted is to get my hands on some money to spend, even if it's other people's. Remember Willard Dodginghorse? He never had a pot to piss in or a window to throw it out of until he got to be manager of that fish-packing plant. Inside of three months he was driving a Buick, moved his family into a new house, and bought three Skidoos."

"Yeah," says Frank. "And that packing plant been broke for close to three years and Willard ain't even had to look for work. They say he put everybody in his family on the payroll, even little Belinda who was only four months old, was drawing $200 a week as a fish-scaler."

"We *could* manage a baseball team," I say.

"We know how to play baseball," says Frank.

"And I saved up $430 once..."

"Before I talk you into going someplace we never been before and spending it all," and Frank laugh.

Lucky we was only five minutes late for the meeting next night, otherwise it would of been over before we got there. Chief Tom been head honcho for so long he got all his friends on the council.

"If Chief Tom says 'Shit!' they all fill their drawers," says Bedelia Coyote. Bedelia like to call herself a watchdog, try to keep the chief from wasting too much money. One time we ganged up with her and stopped him, but the chief can call more meetings than we have the gumption to go to.

"All in favor?" the chief is saying as we come through the door.

"Wait just a minute," yell Bedelia. "I haven't finished discussing the motion. Did you have an accountant study their books? Did you get a lawyer to check on the contract? Did you get a real estate agent to appraise..." and, boy, Bedelia ramble on about five minutes, say all the things I thought about yesterday and a few more besides.

Chief Tom give one of his political answers, which take fifteen minutes or so and don't say one single thing. "I trust this clears up any apprehension you might have about this investment opportunity," he finish up.

"You didn't answer my..."

"Shhh!" I tell Bedelia. "For once in his life Chief Tom is right. Let him be."

Me and Bedelia generally work on the same side, so she eye me up and down from under the blue polka-dot bandana tied around her forehead.

"Trust us," say Frank, smiling. Frank could grin the bark off a tree.

"Well, okay," say Bedelia and sit down.

Chief Tom stare at me and Frank, and if his face was electric we'd be warm as toast.

Soon as the vote pass we sidle up to Chief Tom.

"I know a lot about baseball," I say, "and I study for three years at the Tech School in Wetaskiwin..."

"And I can read and write," says Frank.

"And we'd like to manage this here baseball team," I say. Bedelia curse under her breath and kick over a folding chair.

"Well, young people, I appreciate the offer, but I hardly think you have the financial acumen..."

"We'll work cheap," we tell the chief.

"And it keep us off the streets."

"And if we away from home we don't get any more reserve girls pregnant," say Frank.

"That one move might solve our birth control problems," say Chief Tom, one eye smile just a little bit. That is the closest I ever knew him to make a joke.

"Then you'll hire us?"

"No."

"No?"

"You young people don't understand the workings of the business world," say Chief Tom. "While we do indeed need management personnel for this baseball team, which, incidentally, will henceforth be known as the Montana Indians, there is certain protocol to be followed..."

"What you mean is, the jobs go to your friends."

"There are certain favors to be repaid," say the chief.

"But we got Bedelia off your back tonight. You owe us something."

"Perhaps at a future time..."

"What if we was to promise not to tell Samantha what you was doing last week when we seen you up in Edmonton?"

"But I wasn't doing anything. I had a business meeting at the Four Season's Hotel."

"You know that, and we know that, but what if we told

Samantha we seen you with Mary Big Drum, from the Indian Federation office. She's a pretty woman, single. Bet she'd like to get her hands on a handsome chief..."

"And I bet Samantha's awful hard to live with when she's mad," I say.

"On the other hand," say the chief, "I think you young men have learned one of the secrets of success in business – always have something to hold over your competitor's heads, real or imagined." He puff up his chest and call across the room. "Samantha, dear, I've decided to hire Simon and Frank to manage our new enterprise."

The first inkling I get that things ain't as they should be is from Frank.

"You know, Silas," he say, "that girl in Montana tell me that was the first night she ever work at the ballpark. She say it was the first night any of the food-selling people work there."

My stomach make a little dropping motion, like I was in an elevator.

The second sign I get that maybe we ain't heard the whole story is when an article appear in the *Calgary Herald* the week after us Ermineskin Indians buy that baseball team.

INDIANS RESCUE INDIANS

Edmonton (CP). The financially troubled Montana Magic of the Universal Baseball Association were rescued Friday by the Ermineskin Band of Hobbema, Alberta, and immediately renamed the Montana Indians. Chief Tom Crow-eye of the Ermineskins announced his band had purchased 100% of the stock of the financially troubled team. The Indians, the baseball club that is, lost over $300,000 so far this season.

The Montana Indians players have not been paid for three weeks, and player representative Stanley "Bad News" Ballantine, former major leaguer, says the team will not play until all overdue salaries are paid.

And there is another thing. It seem when we get to Montana that me and Frank ain't replacing anybody. Some lady clerk in the City Light and Power Department been managing the team.

I thought I was the only one never heard of the Universal Baseball Association, but it seem like nobody else ever hear of it too. In the sports section of the daily newspaper it show there are teams in Williston, North Dakota; Casper, Wyoming; Provo, Utah; Carson City, Nevada; and Rapid City, South Dakota – all places that ain't very big, or interesting, or close together.

I don't think most of us, including Chief Tom who think he's so smart, ever heard of the word *affiliation*. That's what the Montana Magic had lost about a month before we bought them.

We find out real quick that the other five teams in the league have what are called *major league affiliations*, and which is why last year the team was called the Montana Cubs. The long and short is that a major league baseball team sponsor the Universal Baseball Association clubs, supply young players, rent a baseball park, supply money for wages, traveling, baseball, uniforms, groundskeepers, and a few dozen other things that we never even thought of.

Without an affiliation we are an independent team and have to pay all our own expenses. It don't take us long to find out there is no way for an independent team to break even. The big league teams *expect* to lose money in places like Montana. The Universal Baseball Association clubs are called farm teams.

"I never seen a farm could slurp up money like this here business," says Frank, after we been there for a week or two. Every mail be full of bills.

And there is never any money coming in.

Lucky for us the team was on the road for the first week we was there, 'cause on the first night they were at home, after we bought up about a ton of food and hired in all the concession people from before, only nine people pay to get into the game.

By asking a lot of questions the next day, I find out that, since the city want to sell the team real bad, Mr. Gino get them to promise a day off with pay to *all* city employees if they go to the baseball game and take their family and friends the night we was brought to the park.

I put in a call to Chief Tom and suggest this here baseball team is like flushing money down the toilet, and we should maybe hire back Mr. Gino and his friends to sell it for us quick.

Chief Tom yell at me for being wasteful. "The statement I have in front of me indicates the club to be a sound financial operation. If you don't keep it that way you'll have to be replaced."

"To start with we need another $100,000 over and above what you give us already just to pay the bills," I say.

"You have a ten-game home stand," say the chief, "use the gate receipts."

I explain about nobody coming to the park.

"Nonsense," say the chief, "perhaps it was just a cold night?" Then he pause for awhile before he say, "Oh, alright, I'll send you $50,000, but then you have to manage with what you take in. It's called the *profit motif*. You have to take in more money than you spend..."

I just about drop the phone on the floor when I hear he going to send me that money. I guess what Bedelia Coyote and other people been telling me is true.

"You guys are so dumb," Bedelia has said to me and my friends more than once. "There's millions of dollars floating around. Chief Tom and the Tribal Council are just dying to spend money. In fact they *have* to spend money. If they don't invest the royalties and Government money, the Government take it back at the end of the year and use it for the Alberta and Saskatchewan Navy."

"Ain't no Navy in Alberta," I say. "Ain't no ocean."

"Don't matter to the Government. There's a Navy in Edmonton. Ship is called HMCS Nonsuch. Only they don't have a ship. Guys just dress up in Navy uniforms and march around in circles on a concrete lot."

"But they won't usually give us $50 when we ask for it."

"If you'd let me handle it we'd have lots of money. First you have to incorporate a society, draw up a constitution, elect officers, set up a project, get Government approval..."

"It's easier to steal..." says Frank, and I have to agree.

With the money Chief Tom send us, me and Frank rent an apartment in town, got two bedrooms, carpet all through, and a squawk box on the door. We bring our girls down from Canada and it is just like a big holiday. Frank want to buy furniture but I say no we should wait for two months see if this baseball team stay in business.

The day that baseball team get back in town two players come in, one ducking his head about a foot to get through the door of the trailer. Frank gone into town; he went to order a little sign to go on each desk in the office, one to say SILAS ERMINESKIN, the other to read J. FRANK FENCE-POST, GENERAL MANAGER.

"I'm Bad News Ballantine," the tall ballplayer say to me, and by his tone of voice I think he expect me to know who he is. I don't hardly follow sport at all, except to read headlines in the *Edmonton Journal*, and *Calgary Herald*, once in awhile.

"And this here's Benny Santiago," and he point to the stocky, dark man who follow him in. "He used to play for the Braves."

I don't have any idea what to say to these guys. I sure wish Frank was here.

"Either of you guys know Wayne Gretzky?" I say, and smile kind of foolish.

"What the hell did he say?" the tall man ask the short man. Mr. Bad News is aoout six-and-a-half feet tall, thin as a pole, have high cheekbones, red hair, and looks as if maybe he got a baseball stuck inside one of his cheeks.

"I'm Silas," I say. I was going to say Mr. Ermineskin, but I just couldn't bring myself to. "What can I do for you?"

He stare at me out of pale blue eyes, and I'm sure he didn't understand a word I said.

"Money," he say, "Moola, dinero, wampum."

"How much and for what?" I say real slow, and clear as I'm able.

"Our paychecks are two weeks overdue, and none of us pick up a bat until we get paid," he say, and the dark man with him nod his head up and down.

"My boss says you was paid up until tomorrow. That's

what the salesman who sold us the team, Mr. Gino..."

"Our last checks bounced higher'n an infield pop-up," says Mr. Bad News.

I take our brand new checkbook out of the desk drawer and try and look like a manager should.

"How much do we owe you, Mr. Bad News?"

"Don't you know?" he say look at me kind of strange.

"Well, the lady who got the records still promising to deliver them..."

He shake his head and glare at me and then name a figure.

"That your salary for the whole year, or maybe two?" It is more money than I ever made in my whole life, even counting five-finger bargains, and all the things Frank creatively borrows.

I guess he can tell I don't believe him, 'cause he whip a sheaf of papers out of his back pocket, toss them down on the desk, turn and spit tobacco juice on the floor of the trailer.

"You just read that, Sonny. That's my contract with the Montana Magic, and you bought it when you bought the team."

I pretend to read all the *whereas* and *heretofore* words, but I can't understand any of it.

"How many players did you say was on this here team?" I ask.

He slap a hand to his forehead. "Why wasn't I happy when I was in the Bigs?" he say. Then to me, "Eighteen. Don't you know nothin'?"

"Do they all make as much money as you?"

"Naw. Me and Santiago here are the stars. The other guys are just scuffles and frauds, and club players."

"That's good," I say, open up the checkbook and write out their checks with my hand hardly shaking at all as I add the three zeroes after the numbers on the check for Mr. Bad

News.

Our Indians play six games that week, lose them all, and the most people to come to a game is on Saturday when sixty-five show up.

The bill for the lights come in and it is also two months overdue and is for more than it take me to live on for a year.

Mr. Bad News Ballantine show up in my office after the last home game, say to me "Where's the bus?"

"What bus?"

"How the hell do you expect us to get to Williston, and then to Rapid City?"

I sure hate to look dumb. But I never thought of how the team traveled.

"Do you think you could call up a bus for me? You been here a while and..."

"You got to book the sonofabitch a week in advance."

"Oh."

"And you got to hire a driver."

"Oh. I figured one of you guys drove."

"We play baseball. Speaking of which, you should have our meal money ready."

"Meal money...?" It turn out that they get $20 a day, each, in cash. And things just keep piling up like that. I have to admit I don't know anything about managing anything, and it ain't near as much fun as I thought to have a sign on my desk with my name in raised-up letters.

We finally rent a yellow school bus, have BROTHER DAVE'S GOSPEL CRUSADE written in blue letters on the side.

"Brother Dave went bankrupt," the rental man say to me.

I have to drive the bus 'cause we can't scare up a driver on short notice. Frank come along for the ride – we tell Connie and Sadie to sit in the office and that it's okay to sign our names to checks if there is bills to pay, or if they need anything for themselves.

Boy, baseball players is about as close to animals as they should be allowed to get and not be kept in cages. About all they do as we creep across the prairies in that oily-smelling school bus, is drink beer, fart, sing dirty songs, and have food fights whenever we stop for meals. They bring about two dozen hamburgers on the bus once, and Bad News Ballantine stand at the back with a bat while a pitcher name of Lumpy throw the burgers and he hit them. One time a half a bun covered in ketchup hit the glass right by my face, slide slow down the windshield, go plop right on the fuel gauge. Frank punch some guy for getting mustard in his hair. And I didn't know I was supposed to make hotel reservations for the team.

When I try to find us a place to stay, I learn that baseball players is about as welcome as Indians at big hotels. In Williston, Mr. Bad News finally direct me to the Gravel Pit Motel, where we settle everybody in for the night in rooms with linoleum floors, and beds with mattresses that sag like hammocks in the middle.

Baseball players also have a hard time getting used to working for Indians.

"Where do you Indians get all of your money?" ask that pitcher named Lumpy.

"We don't really know," I tell him, being honest. "Oil men pay the Government. Government hold our money, check how we going to spend it before they give it to us."

"They can't check very good or you wouldn't own this team," say Bad News. "Whole franchise is about as valuable as a bucket of cold piss."

"Think I could pass for an Indian?" ask Santiago. "I'd like to get my hands on some of your money."

"I used to think that too..." I say.

"We been poor all our life," say Frank. "When I was a kid I was so poor if I didn't wake up in the morning with a hard-on, I didn't have nothing to play with."

On the next road trip I rent us a better bus, but we run out of money on the way back from Nevada.

I try to phone the girls but a telephone lady come on the line to say that our number is no longer in service. I think the telephone bill is one of many I been pushing to the back of my desk. It take all the money we been sent just to pay off the players.

"We don't have any money to buy gas," I tell the players, as we stopped at a truck stop somewhere in Utah.

"Don't look at us," say Bad News Ballantine, after we ask if maybe they'd cough up some of their meal money for gas. They do buy me a meal, and Frank too, though they take a vote on Frank and he only win by a score of 9-8, with one player too passed out to vote.

The players say if they buy gas, they going to head the bus for California, as that the direction most of them live.

I phone the reserve, and over the Tribal Council's phone come Chief Tom's voice, but it be a recorded announcement: "This is Chief Tom Crow-eye speaking, myself and my executive assistant Ms. Yellowknees will be in Europe for the next six weeks where we will be drumming up support for Indian land claims, among potentates of the Scandinavian nations. Please leave a message after the tone."

I managed to squeeze in the word, "Help," before the operator tell me I can't leave no message 'cause nobody is there to accept the charges.

Frank then go for a walk into that Utah town, accompanied by his jackknife. He come back with a four-foot piece of garden hose and while we all drink coffee in the truck stop, Frank he become what Bad News Ballantine call our "designated siphoner."

It don't seem like much use to bring the players back to Montana, but I hate to be responsible for losing them on the road.

Frank finally siphon us all the way back to our ballpark. The first thing the girls say to us is, "They turned off the lights."

That was one bill I really mean to pay, but if I didn't pay wages, there wouldn't of been any players. So what good would the lights have been?

When the players show up for that night's game and find no lights, they corner me and Frank in our office. "Listen, Baitbucket," is how Bad News Ballantine start his conversation with me, and I afraid for a minute that they might do us a certain amount of harm.

"Can't get no blood out of a turnip," Frank tell them, when they complain that their contracts guarantee them travel money to their hometown.

"Yeah, but I bet we could get blood out of an Indian," say Bad News, shake a baseball bat under Frank's nose.

That afternoon we sent Sadie and Connie back to Alberta with Louis' truck.

"How about if you was to help yourself to whatever is loose around here?" I say to the players. And before I even get the words out of my mouth, Bad News Ballantine got the electric typewriter off my desk hugged to him like it was his lost baby. Somebody else get the adding machine, the stapler, and a tall lamp that sit in the corner. Inside of ten minutes the trailer is empty and the players scattered like dandelion fluff. They also carried away their uniforms, balls, bats, even the bases. Seems odd to me but somebody even unscrewed and carried off the toilet seat from the dressing room trailer.

Next day, me and Frank try to salvage whatever we can.

We sell the little concession trailer for $200, and a used lumber dealer take the bleachers and fence off our hands. He come in with a couple of flat-deck trucks and a crew of men and in eight hours everything is gone, even the backstop and the scoreboard.

Early next morning we get waked up by somebody pounding on the door of the trailer. There is two tow trucks outside and a man with a sheaf of legal papers.

He is repossessing the trailer for some bills we owe. I don't bother to ask which ones. We just barely get our clothes on, and take a little food out of the refrigerator. They plant wheels under the trailers, hook on to them, and in only a few minutes there is nothing but a little dust drift a foot or two above the road and ditch.

Everything is real quiet. The sun is bright in the east, sow thistle are golden in the ditches. All that's left is me and Frank, the eight tall silver light poles, and a sky big and empty, where a couple of hawks cruise, so high they look like coat-hangers in the glare.

THE PRACTICAL EDUCATION
OF CONSTABLE B.B. BOBOWSKI

Me and my friend Frank Fencepost have this way of getting into trouble, no matter how hard we try to stay out of it.

I mean we try to avoid making and selling home-brew and moonshine. We figure if people want to do that it is their business. But when the RCMP come around they don't care who they make trouble for, and they *always* coming around, sometimes even with their police dog, Sergeant Cujo. That name ain't a joke, much as we'd like it to be. RCMP really call their tracking dog Sergeant Cujo, and my guess is he really get paid like a sergeant. He is one of these here German Shepherds, mean as three hangovers, drool a lot and show off his big teeth. Constable Chretien, the dumbest RCMP in all Canada, travel with Sergeant Cujo, and the dog sit right up on the front seat of the cruiser, actually have a more intelligent look on his face than Constable Chretien. The dog wear a little brown blanket made of the same stuff as RCMP uniforms and have little sergeant's stripes on his shoulders.

It taken us three years, but we almost got Constable Chretien trained so that he only enforce serious laws, like big thefts, and murders where the dead person didn't deserve to get killed. Constable Greer, the old RCMP who sit all day in his office and smoke his pipe, say "If left alone things will find their own level, and the less we do to disturb the natural level the better."

All RCMPs should be like Constable Greer, especially the new human assistant Constable Chretien have these days. The new constable is a woman, and her being around ain't a pleasure for either us or Constable Chretien. She sign her citations B.B. Bobowski. Don't know if she have names or not. She is right out of RCMP school in Regina, and it said she graduate first in her class because she memorized every law Canada ever had, have, or likely to have, and she feel it her personal duty to enforce every one.

She also got a big mouth; she not only going to clean up all the crime within fifty miles on all sides of Wetaskiwin, she gonna "make women aware of their place in society." Some of the women she mess with is our girlfriends.

"B.B. Bobowski's so damned liberated she rolls her own tampons and kick-starts her vibrator," is what Frank says of her. We sometimes call her Ba Ba Bobowski, and make sheep sounds when we see her coming down the street. Sometimes we put the words together to make *Baba*, which mean grandmother in Ukrainian and I think some other languages too.

Constable Bobowski don't know a thing about water finding its own level. "She gonna drain the lakes and divert the rivers," says Frank.

"She has a five-year career plan," Constable Greer told us, smile real slow, blow pipe smoke at the ceiling; he got sad pouches under his eyes like a dog. "You young people are just going to have to be very patient with her; she's very ambitious."

"We all gonna get to be patient in Drumheller Penitentiary," we say. "She got to learn she can't mind the business of the whole reserve."

Constable B.B. Bobowski make it her personal project to

stamp out home-brew on the reserve. She sniff around out in the dark once and stumble on Maurice Red Crow's still. She run back to Wetaskiwin for reinforcements, but Constable Greer and Constable Chretien both tell her to wait for some serious crime. She go right over their heads to Edmonton, and about forty RCMP's raid the reserve at 4:00 a.m. the next day.

Lucky someone seen Constable Bobowski snooping around. We had time to move the still and also tear the culvert out of the road up to our cabins. We covered the hole in the road with a tarpaulin we borrow off an 18-wheeler was parked at a truck-stop on the highway.

The way we found out about the raid was when Constable Bobowski's car go nose first into the culvert hole, and the car behind ram into her, do themselves about $3000 damage.

For all the rest of that night Constable Bobowski try to find out who to charge for taking the culvert out of the road. She even get the fingerprint man from Wetaskiwin out of bed, have him come and put white powder on that culvert, which is over four feet across and 25 feet long, try to find out whose hands have been on it. Somebody finally point out that since the culvert is on Indian land, moving it don't come under the Highway Traffic Act. Seem that there's no law against us moving our own culvert if and when we want.

"It was moved to prevent a flood," Frank told her.

"This land doesn't flood."

"'Cause we prevent it by moving the culvert."

Constable Bobowski slap her citation book closed, sound like a gun shot. I bet at that point she wished she'd studied to become a librarian or a welder and not an RCMP.

"I doubt if she's going to be superintendent quite as soon as she plans," said Constable Greer the next day. "But you fellows had better watch out. She's mad as a wet hen."

Constable Bobowski don't give up easy. She take Sergeant Cujo away from Constable Chretien and spend a couple of weeks brushing up that dog on how to sniff out alcohol, especially home-brew. Then she bring him to the reserve, where he go sniff-sniffing up the road between the cabins, pull hard on his leash. First thing he do is sniff out a half bottle of stale beer that been left behind a curtain on Mad Etta's window. Then he jump up and go "Bow-wow-wow," right in the face of old Esau Tailfeathers who, folks say, has been drunk since about 1947.

"Smart dog," said Frank. "He found out where we hide the home-brew."

Constable Bobowski, who could be pretty if she was to smile once in a while, stare at Frank like he was a slug leaving a gooey trail on the sidewalk. She has blond hair, cut short and watered on the sides and back to a duck-ass cut, blue eyes, and a flat little nose like a baby.

"You know, Constable Bobowski," Frank say real polite, "I mean what I'm gonna say very respectful. I bet when you take off your uniform you're a real pretty woman."

She squint up one eye and look harsh at Frank again. "When I take off my uniform I'm still a cop. And when you take off your clothes you're still a criminal. And the two don't mix. So don't try to soft-soap me, Fencepost."

"That's cruel," says Frank. "I was just trying to be nice."

"I've heard all about you," say Constable Bobowski.

"Wouldn't you like to find out if it's true or not?"

The constable just look stern and go on with her investigation. That damn dog sniff out Jarvis Lafrenierre's still, and Jarvis end up going for six months to the crowbar hotel in Fort Saskatchewan.

The other people who got stills move them deeper into the woods.

Bunch of us have a meeting at Blue Quills Hall one afternoon, try to figure what to do about Constable Bobowski and Sergeant Cujo.

"We got to stop both the dog and the woman," says Frank.

"You're being too hard on her," says Bedelia Coyote. This is what we expect from Bedelia, 'cause she is about as liberated as the constable. "She sees what a problem alcohol is on the reserve and she wants to stamp it out."

A few people go "Boo."

Bedelia is in a tough spot. She is one of us but she is also a tough woman, and since Constable Bobowski been in Wetaskiwin she helped set up a Rape Crisis Line, and she almost convinced City Council to cough up money for a half-way house for battered women, most of who would come from the reserve.

"I bet Bedelia ratted on Jarvis Lafrenierre," say somebody.

At this point I have to jump in to defend Bedelia, 'cause we know, even if she really mad with us, she wouldn't turn nobody in. No real person would ever do that.

"Can't you explain the facts of life to her?" we say to Bedelia.

"I've tried, but she says the law is the law."

If Constable Bobowski could only understand, trying to stop Indians from cooking up a little home-brew would be about as easy as arresting all the trees on the reserve, handcuffing them, fitting them all into a patrol car and driving them to jail in Wetaskiwin. I imagine Constable Greer must have told her all this, but she apparently ain't gonna let the impossible stop her from trying.

"We got to have a plan," says Maurice Red Crow.

"Which one you figure is smarter, the dog or the lady constable?" asks Frank.

"The dog," everyone shout.

69

That ain't the answer everyone was looking for, but it start Frank to thinking.

Frank decide to become friends with Sergeant Cujo. The sergeant live in a big dog house behind 12-foot chain link fencing, at the rear of RCMP headquarters in Wetaskiwin. Sometimes Sergeant Cujo is on a heavy chain so he can't get to the fence, other times he is free in the yard. When people come by he bark like crazy and run to the end of his chain, or else right up to the fence, stand on his hind legs, snarl and bellow.

Frank spend the first hour just talking soft to the dog. Pretty soon, the dog stop bellowing, stand still with his lips curled back, growl soft in his throat.

"See, he's tame already," and Frank move his hand toward the fence; the sound of Sergeant Cujo's teeth clamping together is like a bear-trap shutting.

"Well, pretty tame," says Frank, as he take a baby bottle from his jacket pocket.

Frank then rub a little hamburger on the nipple, push the nose of the bottle slowly through the fence. Sergeant Cujo sniff the nipple, then lick it good. Frank spend about two hours learning Sergeant Cujo to drink from the bottle what Frank stole from his sister Rebecca's cabin. I bet one of his little nieces is drinking from a cup today.

The bottle is full of home-brew.

After about a week, as soon as Frank come around the corner of the police building, Sergeant Cujo give a friendly "Woof!" and come bounding to the fence. He has developed a real taste for home-brew.

"I bet you got some Cree in you," Frank tell the dog.

Everyday now Frank have to refill the bottle about four times from a jug he keep under the seat of Louis' truck. After four drinks Sergeant Cujo chase his tail a lot, act just as if he was a puppy again.

A few days ago, Constable Greer tell us that Sergeant Cujo bit Constable Bobowski when she come on shift at five o'clock. "We can't understand it," the constable say, "that dog is really irritable these days. We even took him to the vet but he just suggests exercising him more."

We head on downtown, smiling like we just won a lottery.

Frank also don't visit Sergeant Cujo for two days; the two days before Constable Bobowski due to bring him on her weekly patrol of the reserve.

Boy, when she arrive, Sergeant Cujo is skittish as a deer, and he snarl and snuffle like a trail bike as he strain on the leash Constable Bobowski is holding. As they go by Frank's cabin, Sergeant Cujo sniff up about a pound of dirt and jump like he been electric-shocked. He charge the door of Frank's cabin, and when Frank's little sister, Cindy Fencepost open the door the dog knock her down and make footprints the length of her. He break loose from Constable Bobowski, knock over the Fencepost's kitchen table and dive under the bed in the corner where Frank put about 40 ounces of home-brew in one of his mother's baking bowls, and then trailed a few drops out to the road.

While Constable Bobowski search the cabin and try to drag the dog out from under the bed, Frank he pour an ounce or so of home-brew on the seat of the cruiser.

By the time the constable drag the sergeant from under the bed he drank up the evidence. The dog is actually smiling; he stand on his hind legs and hug Frank like a brother.

"What you got here is a dirty old booze-sucking hound," Frank tell the constable as they walk outside.

Sergeant Cujo discover a couple of cases of empty Leth-bridge Pale Ale bottles by the side of the cabin, and he lift each bottle up by the neck, drain out the last few drops.

"Sad," says Frank. "Just like a dog who suck eggs. He's gonna have to go to that big RCMP detachment in the sky."

"Maybe you could teach him to smell out stupidity," yell Frank's mother from the doorway of her cabin. "You and him could be lifelong companions."

Soon as Constable Bobowski let the dog into the cruiser, he go "Woof!" and take a big bite right out of the middle of the front seat. He grin at everybody, kind of woozy-eyed, while upholstery and foam rubber hang from his mouth.

Constable Greer tell us the next day that Sergeant Cujo been transferred to Regina for retraining, or maybe retirement.

"If a dog can get into the RCMP shouldn't be no trouble for him to get into AA," says Frank. Constable Greer crinkle up his face.

"Life will be a lot more relaxed with Sergeant Cujo reassigned," he says. And we agree with him.

But the loss of the dog don't stop Constable Bobowski from popping out from behind trees all over the reserve.

"Remember how dumb she looked the time we pulled out the culvert?" says Maurice Red Crow. "I think the way to get her is to keep feeding her phony information."

In order to do that we got to have an informant. Somebody got to continually rat to the RCMP.

"Can't be just anybody," we say, "got to be somebody who look and act the way the RCMP think a snitch should."

We consider quite a few of our own people, but none of them could ever pretend good enough. There is nobody as low as a snitch. Most people wouldn't even want to pretend they was one, even if the cause was good.

Then somebody think of Peter Lougheed Crow-eye, the

Chief's son.

"He was born lookin' like a snitch," says Frank. And that's true. P.L., as we call him now, is about fifteen, fat and round as if he been filled by the air-hose at Hobbema Texaco Garage.

His father, Chief Tom, left the reserve a few years ago, have an apartment in Wetaskiwin where he live with his girlfriend, Samantha Yellowknees. P.L. always been a sissy, wear suits even when he don't have to. P.L. spend some weekends with Chief Tom, who send him to ballroom dancing lessons at Mde. Ludmilla's Dance Studio in Wetaskiwin. The Chief gave P.L. a copy of *The Rules of Parliamentary Procedure* for his tenth birthday.

Being the kind of guy he is, we were sure surprised a month or so ago when P.L. come into the Hobbema Pool Hall one night. He wearing jeans and a buckskin jacket, both of them new.

He buy three bags of Frito chips, a deck of cigarettes, ask if he can join in on our pool game. We all snicker behind our hands, but we let him, and he turn out to be almost an alright guy.

"My old man the windbag," is how he refer to Chief Tom, and he use some pretty large four-letter words to describe Samantha.

He's still too much of a suck for us to really like him, but as Frank say at the end of the evening, "He got a 50% chance of turning out human."

Now we go to P.L. Crow-eye and ask if he want to do some dangerous work for us. He curl up his lip and say "Sure." But we can tell he's scared as hell.

Next weekend when he go to Wetaskiwin, he wear his suit and dress shoes, and he get his haircut as usual, though he'd planned to start growing his hair long like us. Still smelling of barber shop powder, he go over his lines with us at the Gold Nugget Cafe, then head to the RCMP office to see Constable Bobowski.

"I'm Chief Tom Crow-eye's son, Peter Lougheed Crow-eye, and I want to report a crime," he going to say to Constable Bobowski. Then he going to tell her how much he hate to see liquor on the reserve, praise her for scaring the still owners off the reserve, and tell her how he overheard that a shipment of home-brew coming to Hobbema on the south-bound six o'clock train from Edmonton.

The day before, me and Frank visited Constable Greer and Constable Chretien; they even offer us coffee. Funny, three years ago Constable Chretien wouldn't have done nothing but stick the barrel of his gun up our noses.

"We can't tell you what's going on, but we hear rumors. We suspect Constable Bobowski going to get pretty excited about something tomorrow afternoon," we say.

"And maybe we should let her call in the troops from Edmonton," say Constable Chretien, who been getting smarter every year he study with us.

Peter Lougheed Crow-eye, the snitch, do his job real good and that evening about 25 RCMPs, both plainclothes and uniforms, raid the south-going train when it stop at Hobbema. They search all the freight cars and make all the passengers get off. All they find is three passengers with illegally open liquor on their persons. They write out citations and go away mad. We reckon Constable Bobowski now have two strikes against her.

I heard once, maybe even read it in a book, that if you want to hide something, best place is to put it out in plain sight, only in a spot where people never expect it to be.

Right on the big wooden deck of the railroad station, has been sitting for the last month or two, a tall metal barrel, say

KEROSENE in bright red letters on the side. Old Gertie Big Owl been selling kerosene, either from the station or from Hobbema General Store for years and years. One night we hired George Longvisitor, who own a portable welding rig attached to his truck, to do certain alterations to Gertie's barrel. Now there are two hoses and two sections to the barrel and people who know can buy either kerosene or home-brew.

"If they was to have a taste-test the kerosene would win," says Frank.

But that idea I read in the book really work. If you ain't looking for something, you don't see it. One day Constable Bobowski lean right on the barrel and visit with old Gertie for about half an hour, while Gertie's filling orders for both kinds of kerosene.

My experience is that hardly anybody, anywhere, know what they're doing. The important thing is that they look the part. People listen to suits and uniforms no matter how stupid the advice. That is why Constable Bobowski believe Peter Lougheed Crow-eye when he feed her more bad information: he have that oily, well-fed, shifty-eyed look RCMPs expect from an informant.

P.L. assure Constable Bobowski that Maurice Red Crow, David One-wound, Ovide Powder, and at least two other guys, not only going to ship moonshine to Hobbema, but they traveling with the shipment themselves.

She call straight to Edmonton for assistance again, and by an hour before train time there are more RCMPs than stray dogs on the reserve. Some are carrying rifles, one is even crouched behind the barrel on the station platform, and another is on the roof of the station house.

"They must have watched all the old Jesse James movies just like we did," says Frank.

We was going to sneak some water barrels onto the train

when it stop a few miles up the line at Millet, just to give them a thrill. But if there is one thing we learned years ago it is that RCMPs have no sense of humor.

This time a couple of big cheese RCMPs come down in a chauffeured black car; they sit fifty yards down the street, watch as the train get surrounded from both sides as it pull to a stop.

Later, when everything has quieted down and after the RCMP didn't find a thing, Constable Bobowski get called over to that long, black car. As she walk past the station, Frank and Rufus and a few other guys lean against the station wall going "Ba, ba, ba."

I sure wish I could of heard what was said in that car. The man in the front seat was sort of barking at Constable Bobowski; I bet he ain't gonna lick her face like Sergeant Cujo would of. I guess you can't get demoted down from constable, at least and stay in the force.

After the train, the limousine, and all the other RCMPs have left, I watch as Bedelia Coyote go over to Constable Bobowski's patrol car. I been listening to Bedelia rehearse what she going to say for most of the afternoon.

"You can arrest me if you like," she going to say. "I knew there was no moonshine on that train and so did everybody else on the reserve. You been had. And you gonna keep on being had until you smarten up. You got to learn that if people ain't ready to change laws don't matter a damn.

"You know I ain't got no use for those mealy-mouths from the church, but there's a poster up in Fr. Alphonse's office at the school that say something about changing things that can be changed and accepting things that can't. Well, that poster's a hell of a lot smarter than you..."

Then Bedelia's gonna try to talk her into putting her energy into things she's good at. She even gonna hint the moonshine makers might contribute to the Crisis Line and projects like that.

Bedelia could end up in jail. It hard to figure if Constable Bobowski had enough schooling from us yet or not.

TO LOOK AT THE QUEEN

I been keeping a secret for over a year now. It was one of the conditions that they let us out of jail.

"You must not tell anyone about this for at least a year," a gray-faced Englishman say to us. "There has been quite enough embarrassment of late."

He was a detective with Scotland Yard. I never was able to understand why the English police force was called Scotland Yard. It was in a big stone building, not a yard, and I'm pretty sure it was in London and not Scotland. Though maybe it is like Edmonton being in both Alberta, Canada, and North America.

How me and my friend Frank Fencepost come to get to London, England, is a story itself. I ain't very political. Me and my friends try to keep Chief Tom Crow-eye from ripping us off too badly, and we tangle with the Government over the silly rules they expect us Indians to follow. But I never been involved in this business of aboriginal rights and land claims and all that stuff, and neither have my friends. I don't understand the issues. And I'm pretty sure most of the guys involved, especially the ones who yell the loudest, don't either.

I think the charter flight to London, England, had to do

with both land claims and the new Canadian Constitution. The Constitution is something else I don't understand and don't want to.

Near as I can see a bunch of smart Indians got some Government grants so they could fight the Government. And, as part of the fight, they all decide to go to England, talk to the Parliament there, maybe even get to see the Queen.

Martin Red Dog, from a reserve over near Regina, say to us in the Alice Hotel bar one night, "This trip ain't gonna change anything, but we sure gonna have a hell of a party. And how else is a whole planeful of poor Indians going to get to see England unless the Government pays for it?" And he laugh, show a gold tooth in his long bronze face.

They charter a plane to leave from Vancouver, stop in Calgary, Regina, Winnipeg, and Toronto, before going over the ocean. Going to be 180 Indians from all over Canada, Martin Red Dog tell us.

Chief Tom, though he don't even care about local rights, let alone national or aboriginal, would have liked to go, but him and his girlfriend Samantha Yellowknees already going to Hawaii for a holiday he call a research trip, at Ermineskin Band expense.

Chief Tom name the people from Ermineskin Reserve who get to go on the trip, and he pick his friends Thomas Fire-in-the-draw, Baptiste and Cynthia Wind.

"None of them could tell the Constitution from a trash can," say Bedelia Coyote when she hear. "Their only qualifications is they vote whatever way Chief Tom tell them to."

"That's the way politics work," says Frank Fencepost. "When I get to be dictator I make you a Queen, Silas here a King, and Blind Louis Coyote Prime Minister. Say, which is higher, King or Dictator?"

"Whichever you decide," I say.

The chief couldn't have picked more shifty guys than Thomas Fire-in-the-draw and Baptiste Wind. And Cynthia Wind, I think, is a cousin of Chief Tom. Thomas and Baptiste both wear old suits from the Salvation Army, hang around the reserve do odd jobs for Chief Tom, who slip them Government money some way, but even then they is still mooches, bum cigarettes, food, rides, and booze, even though they supposed to be Christian and belong to the AA.

"You hear about how Baptiste phoned up the AA one night?" says Frank.

I just smile at him knowing he don't need my answer in order to go on.

"'Do you guys take cara drunksh?' he ask. 'Why yes, we do,' say the AA person. 'Do you want to join?' 'No, I want to reshign,' say Baptiste."

"I wonder if they really going to see the Queen?" say Bedelia.

The Queen, I think, is a nice lady, and I wouldn't want to be her. Having people stare at you all day every day, must be worse than having a regular job. The Queen, considering she's white and over 50, ain't near as ugly as she could be. I do wonder though why she lets people dress her the way they do. She always look like pictures of missionaries come to convert us Indians back around 1900.

We seen Prince Phillip, right up close so we could tell he was a real person, when he visit the reserve one time. He seem like a regular guy, and even show he got a sense of humor. When we tell him the buffalo we was going to ride down and kill, keeled over and died of natural causes, he say, "Well, there are some who get awfully nervous about meeting Royalty."

And later on, the Prince say to Chief Tom, "I've heard that the idea for daylight-saving time came from the Indian

Nation."

"Oh, yes," says the Chief, act like he know what's going on, "we Indians are responsible for much of the progress in Canada..." and he talk on for three or four minutes.

The Prince wait for Chief Tom to stop, then say without a trace of a smile, "An old Indian chief set the example by cutting off one end of his blanket and sewing it on the other, to make it longer."

Me and Frank and Bedelia Coyote laugh like crazy when the Prince say that.

Chief Tom is smart enough to realize he been caught in a joke, but he don't know how to handle it. In spite of being red already he blush so much it shows, stutter and look around wishing Samantha Yellowknees was there to rescue him.

"I bet the Queen is more fun than she looks," says Frank. "She probably wears satin underwear and a black garter belt."

Later that night at Mad Etta's it is Frank who suggest we go to England.

"How'd you like to go for a ride in a plane?" he say to Etta.

"Whales don't fly," say Etta.

"How come if I said that you'd knock me through a wall?" I ask Etta, but she just grin and take a swig from her bottle of Lethbridge Pale Ale.

"I'm serious," say Frank. "I know just how to do it. If there's one thing a mooch can't pass up it's free booze."

"You should know," I say.

"Trust me," says Frank. "We can go to England for about $40 worth of liquor."

Everytime Frank says "Trust me," I usually end up in jail somewhere.

But everything go just like Frank expect. The three

Ermineskin delegates spend the night before the plane trip at the Palliser Hotel in Calgary. We meet them in the lobby about six o'clock, and Frank flash a 26-ounce bottle of vodka and say the magic words, "Let's go up to your room and have a drink."

By two in the morning all three of them has gone from happy drunk to roaring drunk to sleepy drunk. Me and Frank been drinking from a rye bottle full of cold tea. We stagger the three of them down to our truck and make sure they is sleeping comfortable before we find a city police officer near the hotel.

"Excuse me, my good man," Frank say to a tall police officer, peering around the rims of the big, bug-eyed, black-rimmed glasses that he wearing. "I have a very sad duty to perform," Frank go on. "There are three of my people outside in a disturbingly disreputable truck, and they are, how should I say, somewhat worse for wear from the effects of alcohol. Being a law-abiding citizen, I feel it my duty to see they don't drive and endanger innocent lives."

The constable look Frank up and down, but boy, in a suit, with his hair combed, and his lips closed over the place where he got teeth missing, Frank look like a banker or a teacher or a minister. In fact, he is clutching the Bible he stole out of Cynthia and Baptiste's hotel room.

"Thank you, we'll look into it," say the constable.

"God bless you, officer. I'm the Reverend Frank, and this is my assistant, Standing-knee-deep-in-running-water, a recent convert to the Lord's work."

"Ummm, yes," say the constable.

"The rehabilitation of our people is one of the most pressing problems facing the Indian Nation these days, don't you agree?"

I move in and tug at Frank's sleeve. I think he is laying it on too thick even if the guy is a policeman.

"Well," says the constable.

"You will be kind to them officer, for they know not what they do."

"We have to catch our plane, Rev. Frank."

"Don't interrupt your evangelist, Standing-hip-deep-in-muddy-water. You don't suppose you could spare a coupla bucks for the Lord's work, do you, officer?"

We is at the airport bright and early, tugging Etta out of the back of a taxi. I'm Thomas Fire-in-the-draw. Etta and Frank is Cynthia and Baptiste Wind. Cynthia's passport don't look anything like Etta, but we count on all Indians looking alike to the customs people.

"I see you have the same last name," a man in a blue uniform say to Frank and Etta. "What relation are you?"

"Wife," says Frank.

"Son," says Etta.

"This is your wife?" say the customs man.

"Any law against liking big ladies?" says Frank.

"You ever had to sleep in an unheated cabin in winter, you'd appreciate me," says Etta. "But my son here is a joker, aren't you, Sonny Boy?" and she crush Frank up against her until I can hear his bones crack.

"Don't be rough, mummy," says Frank through gritted teeth.

Since there's nobody else on the plane from Hobbema, we use our own names. Only other time we have to lie is at the hotel when we claim our friends' reservations.

Martin Red Dog has made contact with lots of politicians and next day we get invited to "an informal reception" at a snooty private club.

I don't know why it should of surprised us, but it did;

politicians in England is just the same as in Canada. They dress fancy, have that overstuffed look about them, and is only interested in "What's in it for them."

The people who form the government, even though they is Conservatives, just like Premier Lougheed in Alberta, don't want to see us.

"We can't do them any good," says Martin Red Dog with a sigh. "You ever notice how it's always the party *out* of power who have a big interest in Indians?"

"We don't have any oppressed ethnic minorities here," a red-faced fellow with a thicker accent than ours begin.

"We used to have Druids," say a hefty, white-haired fellow in the corner, sitting deep on his neck in a leather chair, "but we murdered them all. Frightfully easier than dealing with land claims, and all that folderol."

I think he was joking, but these Englishmen keep such straight faces it hard to tell.

"...but we do have coal miners," the first fellow go on. He wheeze considerably, like he just walked up a flight of stairs. "They are victimized and downtrodden by the industrialists. We thought perhaps you'd care to join one of our demonstrations. We're going to march on 10 Downing Street, Saturday fortnight."

"What did he say?" Frank whisper to me.

"I think he said the miners are going to demonstrate in front of the fort on Saturday night."

We thank the politician for the offer but say we ain't up to demonstrating after our long trip.

That night a couple of guys with their coat collars turned up are leaning in a doorway when me and Frank come out of the hotel to look for a restaurant.

They have sharp, musical accents and it take us a two block walk and through most of dinner before we start to understand their language.

They're from Ireland. All I know about Ireland is that they always bombing each other because they don't like the English. That make as much sense as Canadian politics, so guess things aren't any sillier over here, just a different silliness.

These fellows want us to put in a word for *their* land claim. They explain their problem to us for a couple of hours; we don't understand a word but we sympathize anyway.

"Do ye want to receive some military training?" ask a fellow whose name sound like Shamus, "we could putcha in touch with the Libyans."

"Would that be the Women's Libyans?" ask Frank. "We got trouble with them in Canada, too."

"As far as I can see, being in the military service would be worse than being in jail. I sure wouldn't want to march around wearing a uniform, having some big mean white man telling me what to do," I say.

"Just substitute Indian Affairs Department for Army, and you got our lives now," says Frank.

Shamus don't understand that we making jokes, and he explain Libyans ain't women, but A-rabs who train guerrillas to fight, and make bombs, and hand grenades.

"I didn't know gorillas was that smart," says Frank, and even I ain't sure if he's joking or not.

"Our politicians are so dumb it would be unfair to blow them up," we tell them. "It would be kind of like killing a turkey just because it's stupid."

"And politicians ain't even good to eat," say Frank.

"All fat," I say.

These two Irish guys sure can eat, though, and drink. They put away two meals each and introduce us to dark ale, which taste a little like 10–40 motor oil, and I think cost more.

They leave us with the bill too.

"Forty-one pounds," the waiter tell us.

"Of what?"

"Currency, old sport."

"You sell money by the pound? I collected five pounds of pennies once..."

Together we got $20 Canadian. The waiter ain't looking for kitchen helpers. He call the police even though I try to tell him we got diplomatic impunity, which is something I read about in a newspaper. And Frank say he going to put a curse on the whole restaurant. Frank rub butter on his face, ruffle his hair, paint mustard on his cheeks and dance around the foyer of the restaurant and then down the aisles between the tables.

The police wear blue uniforms, coal-scuttle hats, and are so polite they ain't the least bit of fun. After they take us to jail, one of them phone the hotel and Martin Red Dog come down and get us after he stopped at the restaurant and paid our bill. We borrow all the money Martin Red Dog will loan us, tell him to bill the Ermineskin Band Council, and he promise he will.

We visit some night clubs after that. Frank he collect himself a girl with a bright pink Iroquois haircut.

"We are blood brothers," he tell her while he is trying to take her clothes off in the back of a taxi.

He have to tell the taxi driver about five times that we want to go to the Chomondley Hotel. Finally, the girl break in to say, "The Chumly, luv," and the driver take right off.

"You know the reason I like to ride in taxis?" says Frank. "It's the only time I get to tell a white man where to go."

That pink-headed girl have a friend, but her name is Cecily and she wearing a tweed skirt, high heels, have mousey-colored hair and is going to school to be a librarian. After I tell her I write books and she tell me she reads books, we don't have nothing to say to each other. There must be a law of nature of some kind that an outgoing person – either man or woman – have a friend who is just the opposite, that they drag everywhere, the shy person digging in their heels.

Cecily gets all nervous about going to our hotel, so halfway there we have the taxi driver change directions and go to their apartment, a flat they call it, though it ain't no flatter than any other apartment I ever been to.

Frank and his girl hop right into bed, which is behind a screen have a picture of Japanese soldiers on it. Me and Cecily play dominoes and drink tea at the kitchen table.

From behind the screen the pink-haired girl say something to Frank about birth control.

"Hey, in Canada we got a new contraceptive for men. I use it all the time; it's a pill. I just put it in my shoe. When I walk on it, it makes me limp."

The girls don't want us to stay all night.

"Use my body and then tell me to get lost, you women are all alike," say Frank. His girl don't mind making a date for the next night. Me and Cecily are glad to see the last of each other.

There ain't no taxis around and it is after two in the morning when we get outside.

"Let's walk to the hotel," I say, taking a deep breath of the sweet, foggy air.

"Hey, I know what that is," I say as we walk along, our boots clicking on the stone streets, "that's Buckingham Palace, the place where the Queen lives."

"I bet I could leap right over that fence," says Frank, point at the tall, wrought-iron fence, that is black, about fifteen feet high and have spear points on top of each bar of the fence.

"Not a chance," I say.

"Let me show you," say Frank and look all around. The

streets is deserted and scarves of fog are rubbing around our ankles as we walk. "See all I do is take a run, a jump, grip with my hands and swing myself over into that there hedge."

"No way," I say. But me saying something has never stopped Frank before.

He back clear across the street, pump his feet up and down in one spot for a few seconds, run full speed at that high, black fence. He jump, but not very high, grap on to a bar and swing his body up. He don't rise but halfway up the fence and his body hit parallel to where he gripped and bang hard against the bars. What I see then is that Frank grabbed on to the edge of a hidden gate, and the weight of his body swing a section of fence back into the tall hedge. It make an opening about a foot wide for us to squeeze through.

"That was what I had in mind all along," says Frank. "I got the eyes of an eagle. I seen this here gate all the time."

The Queen's yard is like the biggest park I ever been in. There is lawn enough for a golf course, flower beds galore, and thousands of trees and shrubs. We stroll around for awhile.

"Look!" say Frank, as the palace loom up in front of us, dark gray, against a pale sky that already thinking about morning.

We walk past a place where there is about a hundred wide steps going up to somewhere. Just past those stairs is a little door, like one to a basement. Frank step down into the doorwell and try the handle. The door open.

"Come on," say Frank.

"I don't think we ought to be here," I say.

The palace is dark and quiet and our boots sound like we walking inside an empty oil drum.

The floors is either marble or carpet thick as muskeg, and the whole place smell of velvet, just like a theater. There are tiny lights high up on the walls, which are all twenty feet or more high, covered in wallpaper, tapestry, or stuff look like carpet. There are pictures all over the place, most of dark scenes of men in riding clothes, or men wearing white wigs. There are little tables in the hall have vases or glass ornaments on them.

We climb up a few floors, then down, then up. I wonder if we'll ever find our way out.

Frank he peek into a room now and then, flip on the light, then flip it off.

"This here must be a hotel, Silas," he says and I have to agree. Once I walk through the Empress Hotel in Victoria and this is about the same except the furniture is more expensive and there's more of it.

"Maybe it's the hotel part of the palace, or maybe this is what palaces is like."

Frank push open a door have a crest shaped like the Queen's hat glued to it, and turn on the light.

"Wow, look at that!" say Frank. What he is staring at is a light fixture I bet is made of real diamonds. They dazzle up my eyes and make bug-like shadows of brightness on the walls.

"Shhh," I say, and point to the bed, what covered in a silky blue spread. "Those bedcovers got a lump under them."

But I'm too late. The lump move, sit up, and even though I flick off the overhead light, must of seen us, cause I seen her. I feel like the first time I ever get arrested, like my blood is squishing along real fast and like there's ants on the back of my neck.

"Excuse me," a very English voice say out of the darkness.

"We was just on our way out," say Frank, trip over something, make a loud stumble.

There is a little click and a bedside lamp come on. I am

standing by the door, my hand still on the light switch, Frank has fallen over a coffee table, is just getting up, holding at least one of his ankles.

"Whatever are you doing here?" say the Queen; she got her hair in plastic rollers, just like a real person, and I guess what I notice most is that she is small, maybe only 5'2" or so. I always thought of her as being about seven feet tall. She got her nightgown pulled together at her neck with one hand.

"You don't have to be afraid of us, Mrs. Queen. We was just passing by and thought we'd drop in," I say.

"Yes, well, you...ah...needn't be afraid of me either. In fact, you could call me...or...do you have names?"

"Sure. You can call me Chief Frank," says Frank. "And this here is my friend Silas Ermineskin. Silas has had a book printed up."

"Four books," I say.

"How interesting," say the Queen.

"Yeah, I'm one of the better known chiefs in Canada," says Frank. "A real big wheel. Like if they was to have a King among Indians..."

"He's exaggerating just a little," I say.

"You're not terrorists then..." and the Queen let out a big breath of air.

"Constable Greer of the RCMP call me a holy terror one time," say Frank.

"We flew over here from Canada to see about the Constitution. Our leaders was hoping to see you..."

"I don't think this is the time or the place..."

"We just find our way in here by accident. We was sightseeing. We is really sorry to disturb you..."

"I think perhaps you'd better be going..."

"It must be really fun to be Queen, eh? Being able to

do anything you want and all..." say Frank sitting down on the end of the Queen's bed.

"It's not exactly all that it's cracked up to be," the Queen say in a wistful voice.

"But you're rich. I seen you riding in cars big as house trailers...and they put down carpet for you...and you travel."

"Believe me, ah, Frank, Chief Frank, there are disadvantages..."

"I'd trade places with you."

"I wonder for how long?" and even in the bad light from the bedside lamp I can see the Queen make a sad little smile. "Where have you and your friend been today, Frank?"

Frank pause for a minute try to gather together his thoughts.

"All over. I can't remember all the places, but we walked about twenty miles, I bet. Seen parks and old buildings, and ships in the harbor, and we ate lunch at a restaurant where they wrap my food in a newspaper. Just tonight we been to three nightclubs, for supper we ate grapes at the Hare Krishna's house, and they wanted us to shave our heads..."

"You know, Frank, if you were King, you wouldn't be able to do any of those things...at least not without thousands of people and reporters and television crews following you around."

"I was on the TV once; I liked it."

"I wonder if you'd like to be on the telly every day of your life, and have the whole world waiting for you to make a mistake, spill your food, say something embarrassing..."

"Hey, I do all those things everyday, right, Silas?"

"That's true," I say.

"I'm sure you do. But you couldn't anymore, if you were King. People expect their leaders to be perfect. If you stumble and spill, and say foolish things, if you show emotion, if you get cross, or angry or impatient, people lose respect for you..."

Frank, he light up a cigarette.

"Would you mind?" the Queen say, nod toward the package Frank about to return to his shirt pocket.

"You smoke?"

The Queen's eyes flash across Frank's surprised face.

"Are you shocked?"

"Well, no," say Frank, hold out his package to the Queen, then light a cigarette for her. "It just that you're the Queen."

"I don't smoke in public, but this *is* my home."

"Why don't you smoke in public?"

"People don't expect us to be human."

"But most ordinary people smoke."

"That doesn't make any difference."

I know what she means, but I can't explain it. People who come to interview me or talk about my books are surprised to find I'm just an ordinary Indian. I don't know if they expect me to have wings or feathers, but they want me to be different.

I remember once me and my littlest sister Delores was in the Safeway grocery store in Wetaskiwin when we meet Miss McNeil, Delores' grade-one teacher. Miss McNeil have a basketful of groceries.

"Oh, Miss McNeil," Delores say, "do you eat?"

"Where's Prince Phillip?" ask Frank. "He off traveling somewhere?"

"No. His room is several doors down the hall."

"Do the public expect you not to have sex either, just because you is Queen? Boy, you'd never get me to be King if that's true..."

"Well, if we have sex, we certainly must never mention it. But Phillip and I just find it more comfortable to have

92

separate bedrooms."

"I'm glad we didn't open up Prince Phillip's door by accident," say Frank. "I bet he would have punched us out. Maybe he even sleep with a sword under his pillow."

"We met Prince Phillip once," I say. "Bet he'd even remember us. He come right to Hobbema Reserve and we stage a buffalo hunt for him only our buffalo sort of died of old age..."

"Oh, yes," say the Queen, and she laugh right out loud. She got a real pretty laugh. "The prince regales everyone with that story. I wish I'd been there. You have no idea how boring most social occasions are, everyone tip-toeing around, whispering, afraid everything won't go smoothly. The Prince and I have very pleasant memories of our visits to Canada."

"It gets so cold in Canada the politicians walk around with their hands in their own pockets," says Frank.

"That's another thing you couldn't do if you were King, Frank, is express your opinion. We of the royalty have to remain neutral, that way everyone is able to fantasize that we're on their side, no matter what the disagreement or argument may be about."

We visit for a while longer, until Frank notice the Queen yawn. Then he say, "Well, I guess we should get moving. We're keeping you up and all. And I've decided I won't be King of Canada even when they ask me to."

"Yes, I suppose you have other things to do, and I do have a rather busy day tomorrow. But...just one other thing. The Prince mentioned a...how shall I put this delicately? A rather enormous..."

"Mad Etta," we say.

"Yes, the Prince was very impressed by her..."

"She's here with us," I say. "Etta's traveling incogmento, but you might reach her at the Chomondley Hotel, if you was to ask for Cynthia Wind."

The Queen has got out of bed and put on flowered slippers and a Chinese-looking robe. She walk across the room and open a door that among her shelf of books, and there is a little bar. She take down three small, pot-bellied glasses what was hanging upside down like bats on a wooden rack, and she splash liquor in all three. I can tell by the smell it is brandy.

"Good luck," say the Queen, raise her glass to us.

"To the Queen," say Frank, and we all three touch glasses, making the sound like the first notes of a bell chiming.

"You should make sure you keep the doors closed at night," says Frank. "Otherwise just anybody could walk in here."

"I'll remember that," say the Queen.

"Nice talking with you," I say.

"My pleasure," say the Queen. She smile at us, and I think she mean it.

We close her door real quiet.

We would've got out without disturbing anybody, I think, if Frank hadn't decided to take home a souvenir. He pick up a long-necked vase the color of winter smoke, and as he go to put it under his jacket, it slip right through his fingers, crash in a thousand pieces on the stone floor. Guess the sound wake up whoever was supposed to be guarding the palace.

Boy, in less than half a minute, I bet we is surrounded by a whole army of policemen. We sort of get carried along just like we was in a big crowd that was going someplace.

"I feel like I been rode hard and put away wet," says Frank.

We get asked questions for hours and hours, when all we'd like to do is get some sleep.

Turn out some of them men from Scotland Yard been following us and they seen us having dinner with those Irish guys and figure sure we was there to hurt the Queen.

Neither of us say we talked with the Queen, we think they might execute us or something if they found that out. Besides, the way these men talk, the Queen might get into trouble for visiting with us.

Our pictures is all over the newspaper the next day:

INDIANS ARRESTED
INSIDE
BUCKINGHAM PALACE

Full Investigation Of Palace
Security Underway

Canadian Indians, Thomas
Fire-in-the-draw and Baptiste
Wind were arrested at 3:30
a.m. inside Buckingham...

By the end of the day that information work its way back to Canada where the real Thomas Fire-in-the-draw and Baptiste Wind, who I guess by now is over their hangovers, show up on TV saying they ain't never set foot out of Alberta in their lives.

The next morning, the police take us to a big room where, along with all the pink-faced Englishmen, are three or four small dark men. These men speak to me and Frank in languages, sound as if they spitting out tacks and paper clips. The Englishmen talk among themselves as if we didn't understand English. They are trying to decide if we are Libyan, Iranian or Iraqi terrorists. Then to make matters worse, the Palestinian Liberation Organization claim credit for us, say we was there to blow up the Queen.

"We is just poor Indians from Canada, got lost on our way back to our hotel."

"Can you prove it?"

"Mad Etta," we both say. They bring in Etta, but she ain't who she says she is either, so they just put her in a cell next to ours.

I finally remember fingerprints. "We all been arrested in Canada, plenty of times," I say. "If you was to send our fingerprints to the Alberta RCMP..."

"Or B.C. or Saskatchewan," say Frank, "or North Dakota or Utah."

"That will be quite enough, thank you," say the English detective.

I never thought being arrested by the RCMP would turn out to be a good thing. But our fingerprints prove out who we is.

Just as they about to let us go, Frank breaks the news to them that him and me had a drink and a smoke with the Queen. They don't believe us.

But after we describe the inside of the Queen's bedroom for them, they just kind of slump down in their chairs. I guess they can see themselves losing their jobs.

That's when the head of palace security say to us that if he "cuts the red tape," and send us home to Canada right away, we got to promise not to mention seeing the Queen for at least a year.

I bet we home in Alberta for a month before Etta tell us that the morning after me and Frank arrested, the Queen invite her for tea, all by herself. The rest of the chiefs and the big wheels in their blue suits get to stay at the hotel. "A guy who look like an undertaker deliver the invite in a cream-colored envelope as thick as cardboard," say Etta. "They even send to the hotel, instead of a limousine, a van, where the whole side roll open and Etta able to waddle right inside without all the hassle of pushing and pulling."

She was at the palace for over two hours.

"What did you talk about?" we all ask.

Etta smile in that secretive way she have when she know something the rest of us don't.

"You wouldn't be interested," say Etta. "Just women talk. Us women in positions of power have unusual kinds of problems."

THE INDIAN NATION
CULTURAL EXCHANGE PROGRAM

Every once in a while the Government tries to do something nice for us Indians. Usually it is just before an election when that *something nice* is announced. Whether it ever come about or not is another matter. Sometimes they announce a new program, then after the newspapers get tired of writing about it, they file it away, hope no Indian will ever apply.

That is the way it was with the The Indian Nation Cultural Exchange Program.

OTTAWA TO SPEND
TEN MILLION
ON WESTERN INDIANS

was how the *Edmonton Journal* headline the story, and right up until the election, whenever some sneaky looking politician from Ottawa speak within 50 miles of any Indian Reserve west of Ontario, he mention the program and the amount but be pretty vague about the details. He know that after the election that program get filed deep in a Government vault somewhere.

That would have happened to the Indian Nation Cultural Exchange Program if it weren't for Bedelia Coyote. Bedelia is famous for causing the Government grief. Not that they don't deserve it. One time the Government send 52 John Deere manure spreaders to our reserve. Nobody asked for them, and hardly anybody farm enough to want or need one. Some of my friends try to strip them down as if they were cars, but nobody want to buy the loose parts. Eventually a few of them disappear, the way a cattle herd get smaller if it ain't tended. All that happen maybe eight years ago and there are still eight or ten manure spreaders rusting in the slough below our cabins.

"They should have sent us 52 politicians," say Bedelia. "They're all born knowing how to spread manure. It keep them busy and they be doing something useful for the first time in their lives."

"Even crime wouldn't pay if the Government ran it," say our medicine lady, Mad Etta.

It is Bedelia who go to the Wetaskiwin office of our Federal Member of Parliament, a Mr. J. William Oberholtzer.

"The Conservative Party could run a dog here in Alberta and win by 10,000 votes," I say.

"J. William is about two points smarter than most dogs," says Bedelia. "I seen him tie his own shoes one day. Most politicians don't have that much coordination."

Bedelia have to go back to Mr. Oberholtzer's office every day for about three months, and she have to fill out a whole sheaf of forms, but finally they have to give her the details of the Indian Nation Cultural Exchange Program. Turn out that three people, under 25-years old, from each reserve in Western Canada, can visit another reserve at least 250 miles away to learn the other tribe's culture and teach them about their culture.

"I'll teach them how to drink," says my friend Frank Fencepost. "That's part of our culture, ain't it?"

"Unfortunately," say Bedelia.

"I don't know," says Frank, screw up his face. "I can't drink like I used to. Used to be I could really put it away. But now fifteen or twenty beers and I'm right out of it," and he laugh deep in his chest, sound like someone pounding on a drum. "Maybe I teach them how to have sex appeal instead."

"And I'll demonstrate brain surgery," says Bedelia.

"Yeah, you're right," says Frank. "Can't teach other people to be sexy – you either got it or you ain't."

"Bedelia is a little like the wind," our medicine lady, Mad Etta say, "she slow but steady – wind wear down even mountains eventually."

Bedelia fill out another ton of forms and finally all the papers arrive for people from our reserve to apply to go somewhere else. We get out a map of Canada and try to decide where it is we'd like to go.

"How about California?" says Frank. "I hear they got good weather and pretty girls down there."

"California ain't in Canada," we say.

"Then we'll go down there and talk them into joining up with us."

We argue for a long time about different places, but we know we going to where Bedelia decide, because she done all the work so far.

"You guys ever been to the Land of the Midnight Sun?" Bedelia ask.

"We been to Las Vegas," says Frank.

Bedelia's look is so cold it could freeze us both solid.

"I'm talking about the Arctic. There's a place on the map called Pandemonium Bay, only 300 miles from the North Pole. There's an Indian Reserve there and I think that's where we ought to go."

Like Frank, I'd a lot rather go where it's hot. But I smile at

Bedelia and say, "We're with you." I mean, how many times does the Government do favors for poor Indians?

I remember another time the Government decide to do us Indians a favor. Someone in Ottawa get the notion that we all need new running shoes. Everyone on the reserve. Someone must of told them that Indians like running shoes, or that we all barefoot.

To save money they do the project by mail. Everyone on the reserve get a letter, a big, brown envelope that have a five-foot-long sheet of white paper about two feet wide, folded up in it. Instructions are that everyone is supposed to trace the outline of their right foot on the paper and send it to Indian Affairs Department in Ottawa. Then they supposed to send everyone their running shoes.

We have more fun laughing over the idea than the time we move Ovide Letellier's outhouse forward about ten feet, so when he go to park his brand new Buick behind it, the car fall nose first into the hole.

There are really over twenty people in Louis Coyote's family, and there is hardly enough room to get all the right feet on the paper. The kids draw around feet with pencils, pens, crayons, finger-paint, peanut butter, Roger's Golden Syrup, and 10–40 Motor oil. Some people leave their shoes on; others take them off.

Frank Fencepost draw around a foot of Louis Coyote's horse, and of his own dog, Guy Lafleur. When the running shoes come in the mail, Smokey Coyote get four short, fat shoes, and Guy Lafleur Fencepost two pairs of tiny-baby ones.

When the Government give you something, you got to take it. Mad Etta she put that length of paper on the floor to use as a doormat. The Government write her three letters, say she got to trace her foot and send it to them. Finally they send her a letter say she liable to a $500 fine and 60 days in jail if she don't do as she's told. Mad Etta sit down on a sheet of paper, trace one of her cheeks, and mail it off. A month or two later come a letter say they only make shoes up to Size 32, and her foot is a Size 57.

The kids use running shoes for footballs. We use them for fillers on the corduroy road across the slough. We tie laces together and toss them in the air until the telephone and telegraph lines along the highway decorated pretty good. For years there was faded and rotting running shoes hang from those lines like bird skeletons.

Me, Frank and Bedelia put in applications under the Indian Nation Cultural Exchange Program, to visit Pandemonium Bay Reserve, Northwest Territories.

"Pandemonium Bay has the worst climate and the worst economy in Canada," say Mr. Nichols, my teacher and counselor at the Tech School in Wetaskiwin, after I tell him where we're going.

He go on to tell me it is almost always below zero there, and in real temperature too, not this phony Celsius nobody understands. And he say it snow in July and August, which is their nicest weather of the year.

"The ground never thaws, ever," say Mr. Nichols.

"But I bet the nights is six months long," say Frank. "I don't mind that at all. In that country when you talk a girl into staying the night, she stays the night."

It is the better part of a year before the money comes through. We are the only people ever apply under the Indian Nation Cultural Exchange Program, so everybody make a big deal out of it. There is a picture in the *Wetaskiwin Times* of some suits from the Department of Indian Affairs, present Bedelia with the check. Me and Frank are there, me looking worried, my black hat pulled low, my braids touching my shoulders. Frank grin big for the camera. And of course Chief Tom is there, stick his big face in the picture. He discourage Bedelia every step of the way, but when the time come he take as much credit for what she done as he dare to.

Bedelia is serious about almost everything. She belong to so many organizations I don't know if she can keep track. There is Save the Whales, Free the Prisoners, Stop the Missiles, Help the Seals, Stop Acid Rain, and I bet ten more. If there is anything to protest within 200 miles, Bedelia is there. She is stocky built, with her hair parted down the middle; she wear jeans, boots, and lumberjack shirts, and she thinks I should write political manifestos, whatever they are, and that I should put a lot more social commentary in my stories.

"My motto is 'Piss in the ocean'," Frank tell her when she start on one of her lectures.

In a joke shop one time I found a little button that say "Nuke the Whales" and that about turn Bedelia blue with anger. But she means well even if she's pushy. And she's a good friend.

People is sure odd. Soon as everyone knows where we're going, they start to say, "Why them?" and "Aren't there a lot of people who deserve to go more?"

"If people had their way they'd send two chicken dancers and a hockey player," says Frank. "And how come none of them ever thought of applying to go?" It is true that none of the three of us dance, sing, make beadwork, belong to a church, or play hockey.

To get to Pandemonium Bay we fly in a big plane to Yellowknife, then make about ten stops in a small plane, been made, I think, by glueing together old sardine cans. The plane feel like it powered by a lawn mower motor; inside it is

as cold as outside, and there is cracks around the windows
and doors let in the frost and snow. The pilot wear a heavy
parka and boots, have a full beard make him look a lot like a
bear. And he only growl when Frank ask him a lot of
questions.

Pandemonium Bay is like the worst part of the prairies in
winter, magnified ten times. Even though it is spring it is 30
below.

"Looks like we're on the moon," says Frank, stare at the
pale white sky and endless frozen muskeg.

"Looks just like home," says Bedelia, sarcastic like, point
to some burned-out cars, boarded-up houses, and dead
bodies of Skidoos scattered about. There are gray and brown
husky dogs with long hair, huddled in the snowbanks, puff
out frosty breath at us, while a few ravens with bent feathers
caw, and pick at the bright garbage scattered most
everywhere.

Though the Government make a big deal out of our going,
pioneers they call us in some of their handouts, and send about
twenty pounds of propaganda to Pandemonium Bay, with
copies to each of us, Chief Tom, Mr. J. William Oberholtzer,
Premier Lougheed, and goodness knows who else, there is
only one person meet our plane.

But when we see who it is, it explain a whole lot of things,
like why Bedelia has told us at least a hundred times that we
don't have to go with her unless we really want to, and that
she could get a couple of her demonstrator friends to travel
with her, or even go by herself.

"There won't be much for you guys to do up there,"
Bedelia said, like she wished we weren't going.

"Hey, we make our own fun. I never been arrested in the
Northwest Territories," said Frank.

The only person who meet the plane is Myron Oglala.

Myron, he is the only man Bedelia ever been interested in. He is a social worker and she met him at a Crush the Cruise demonstration in Edmonton a year or two ago, and bring him home with her for a few days. Bedelia never had a boyfriend before, so that sure surprise us all. "A woman needs a man like a fish needs a bicycle," is one of Bedelia's favorite sayings.

Myron is soft and wispy, have a handshake like a soft fruit, and, though he claims to be a full-blooded Indian, is going bald. If you ever notice, 99 out of 100 Indians, even real old ones, have a full head of hair. That is something we is real proud of. We call Bedelia's friend, Myron the Eagle, which we lead him to believe is a compliment, though Bedelia know the truth.

She was as proud of Myron as a mother cat carrying a kitten by the back of its neck. And she explain to us when we get too nasty with our teasing, that her and Myron have an *intellectual communion* with one another.

"I bet you can't buy that kind at the Catholic Church," I say.

"Right," says Frank, "that's why you and him spend fifteen hours a day in your bedroom with the door closed."

Bedelia just stomp away angry. "No reason you shouldn't have sex like everybody else," we say. "But with *Myron*?" And we roll around on the floor with laughter.

Bedelia did admit one day not long after that, that if she was ever to have a baby she'd name it Margaret Atwood Coyote.

We knew Myron was up north somewhere, but we didn't know where, or guess how badly Bedelia wanted to see him again.

"Well, if it ain't Myron the Eagle," says Frank. Myron stare at us through his Coke-bottle glasses, not too sure who we are. I sure hope he recognize Bedelia.

But we don't have to worry about that. Bedelia hug Myron to her, spin him around. She show more emotion than I ever seen from her, except when she's mad at someone.

Myron is expecting us. He have a Department of Indian Affairs station wagon and he drive us a few blocks to what look like a super highrise apartment.

"What's that?" we ask. That huge, semicircular building sit on the very edge of this tiny village, look like something out of a science fiction movie.

"Pandemonium Bay is an accident," say Myron. "Somebody couldn't read their compass, so they built a weather station here when it was supposed to go 600 miles up the pike. By the time somebody pointed out the mistake they'd already bulldozed out an airport, there was so much money tied up they had to leave this town where it was. Bureaucrats from Ottawa, who had never been north of Winnipeg, hired a town planner from New York to build a town for 3000 people. He designed and built this...." What is in front of us is a ten-story, horseshoe-shaped apartment building.

"There was supposed to be a shopping center inside the horseshoe, the stores protected from the wind by the apartments. But there's never been more than 150 people here, ever," Myron Oglala go on.

"I guess it ain't very cold in New York, 'cause the architect installed an underground sewage disposal system, so environmentally sound it would even make Bedelia happy," and Myron smile from under his glasses. It is the first hint we have that he has a sense of humor.

"The sewer system froze and stayed frozen. Indian Affairs spent a few million thawing pipes and wrapping them in pink insulation, but they stayed frozen. The big problem is the pipes are all in the north wall where it's about 60 below all year round," and Myron laugh, and when he do so do the rest of us.

"Folks still live in the first floor apartments. They put in peat-burning stoves, cut a hole in the bathroom floor, put the toilet seat on a five-gallon oil drum, use the basement to store frozen waste."

"Native ingenuity," says Frank.

"Common sense," says Myron, "something nobody in Ottawa has."

Me and Frank get to stay in one of those apartments. The Danish furniture is beat to rat shit, but there are two beds, with about a ton of blankets on each. Four brothers with a last name sound like Ammakar, share the next-door rooms. We find them sitting on the floor in a semi-circle around their TV set. They are all dressed in parkas and mukluks.

"Don't you guys ever take off those heavy clothes?" ask Frank.

"You don't understand," say the oldest brother, whose name is George, then he talk real fast in his language to Myron.

"George says the local people have evolved over the years until they are born in Hudson Bay parkas and mukluks."

All four brothers smile, showing a lot of white teeth.

These Indians seem more like Eskimos to me. They is wide-built and not very tall with lean faces and eyes look more Japanese than Indian. They are happy to see visitors though, and they bring out a stone crock and offer us a drink.

"This stuff taste like propane gas," say Frank in a whisper, after his first slug from the bottle. The four Ammakar brothers smile, chug-a-lug a long drink from the crock, wipe their chins with the backs of their hands. They speak their language and we speak Cree, so to communicate we use a few signs and a few words of English. The drink we find out is called walrus milk. And if I understand what the Ammakars is saying, after two swigs you likely to go out and mate with a walrus.

They sit on the floor of their apartment cross-legged, even though the place is furnished. Ben Ammakar bring out a bag of bone squares and triangles, got designs carved on them. He toss them on the blanket like dice. Him and his brothers play a game that is kind of a complicated dominoes. They play for money. Frank, he watch for a while then say to me in Cree, "This is easy. Boy I'll have these guys cleaned out in an hour. Which pair of their mukluks you like best? I'll win one pair for each of us." Frank draw his cash from his pocket and sign that he want in on the game. I put up a quarter twice and lose each time, though I don't understand the game the way Frank does. I decide to go back to our place. I've never liked games very much anyways. Frank has already won three or four dollars and is so excited he practically glowing. Bet his feet can feel those warm mukluks on them.

I watch television in our apartment. There is a satellite dish on the roof of the apartment and they get more channels than the Chateau Lacombe Hotel in Edmonton.

Earlier, when I mention the big, frost-colored satellite to Myron Oglala, he laugh and tell about how local people react to the television shows.

"*The Muppet Show* is the most detested show on TV," he say, and the character everybody loathe most is Kermit the Frog. In local frog lore the frog is feared and hated. Frogs are supposed to suck blood and be able to make pacts with devil spirits."

"It really is no fun being green," says Frank.

"I bet the people who make *The Muppet Show* would sure be surprised at a reaction like that," I say.

"Up here they call the TV set *koosapachigan*, it's the word for the "shaking tent" where medicine men conjure up spirits, living and dead. A lot of people fear the spirits of the TV are stealing their minds," says Myron.

"Just like on the prairies," says Frank.

About midnight I hear Frank at the door. He come in in a cloud of steam, take off his big boots and hand them out the door to somebody I can't see.

"I lost everything but my name," says Frank, hand my boots out the door before I can stop him.

"I only lost 50 cents," I say, feeling kind of righteous.

"Yeah, but I know how to gamble," says Frank.

To get our boots back Frank have to agree to do a day's work for Bobby Ammakar.

I don't like the idea of working. Just walking around Pandemonium Bay can be dangerous. Without no warning at all ice storms can blow up, and all of a sudden you can't see your own shoes, let alone the house you're headed to.

Bedelia and Myron spend all their time together. There ain't nothing for Frank and me to do except watch TV. This is about the worst holiday I can imagine. Also, nobody is interested in learn about our culture, and these Indians don't have much of any that I can see.

"They worship the Skidoo," says Frank. "At least everywhere you look there's a couple of guys down on their knees in front of one."

"You want to learn about our culture?" says Bobby Ammakar, "we take you guys on a caribou hunt."

And before we can say hunting ain't one of our big interests in life, the Ammakar brothers loaned us back our boots, and we is each on the back end of a Skidoo bouncing over the tundra until there ain't nothing in sight in any direction except clouds of frosty air.

Ben Ammakar is in front of me, booting the Skidoo across the ice fast as it will go, and, when I look over my shoulder, I see we lost sight of Frank and whoever driving his Skidoo. After about an hour we park in the shadow of a snowbank look like a mountain of soft ice cream. I think it is only about three in the afternoon, but it already dark, and once when the sky cleared for a minute, I seen stars. The wind sting like saplings slapping my face, and my parka is too thin for this kind of weather.

When I go to speak, Ben Ammakar shush me, point for me to look over top of the snowbank. Sure enough, when I do, out there on the tundra is a dozen or so caribou, grazing on whatever it is they eat among all the snow and rocks.

Ben take his rifle from its scabbard and smile. He take a smaller rifle from somewhere under his feet and offer it to me.

"I'd miss," I whisper.

If Frank were here he'd grab it up and say, "Fencepost has the eye of an eagle," then probably shoot himself in the foot.

Ben take aim, squeeze off two shots, and drop two caribou, the second one before he do anything more than raise up his head; he don't even take one step toward getting away. The other caribou gallop off into the purplish fog.

"You're a great shot," I say.

"You learn to shoot straight when your life depend on it," says Ben. "If you could shoot we'd have had four caribou."

"You speak more English every time I see you."

"We didn't know if you guys were real people or not. We thought maybe you were government spies." We have a good laugh about that. I tell him how, back at Hobbema we been doing the same thing to strangers all our lives. "But if we'd of killed four caribou, how'd we ever carry all the meat back?" I ask.

"Where you figure the dead caribou is gonna go?" ask Ben.

"And they don't spoil in this here weather."

"Polar bears?" I say.

"Not this time of year; they go where it's warm."

Ben climb on the Skidoo and turn the key, but all that come out is a lot of high-pitched whining and screeching, like a big dog been shot in the paw. At the same time one of them ice storms sweep down on us so we can't see even three feet away. The wind blow ice grains into our faces like darts. Ben take a quick glance at me to see if I'm worried and I guess he can tell I am. My insides feel tingly, like the first time an RCMP pulled my hands behind my back to handcuff me.

"Get down behind here," Ben yell, point for me to let the Skidoo shield me from the wind. He get on his knees above the motor, push a wire here, rattle a bolt there.

"I know some mechanics," I say. "I study how to fix tractors for two years now."

I get up on my knees and look at the motor. I take off one glove, but the tips of two fingers freeze as soon as I do. I think my nose is froze too.

"I think the fuel line is froze up," I say.

I wish Mad Etta was here. It hard to be scared with a 400 lb. lady beside you. Also Etta would be like having along a portable potbellied stove. Etta like to joke that if she was on a plane crashed in the wilderness that stayed lost for six months, everyone else would be dead of starvation but she would still weigh 400 lbs. It true that Etta don't eat like the three or four people she is as big as.

The wind get stronger. The Skidoo motor ice cold now.

"Are we gonna die?" I say to Ben Ammakar.

"You can if you want to," says Ben, "but I got other ideas." I don't think he meant that to be unkind. I sure wish I never heard of Pandemonium Bay and the Indian Nation Cultural Exchange Program.

"Come on," say Ben, stand to a crouch, move around the end of the Skidoo.

"We can't walk out," I yell. "At least I can't; my clothes are too thin."

"Be quiet and follow me," says Ben. I sure wish I had his leather clothes. I didn't even bring my downfill jacket; I didn't expect to be outdoors so much.

I grab onto the tail of Ben's parka and stumble over the uneven tundra. We aren't even going in the direction we come from. The wind is so bad we have to keep our eyes mostly shut. I don't know how Ben can tell what direction we're going in, but in a couple of minutes we stumble right into the first dead caribou. Ben whip a crescent-bladed knife out from somewhere on his body, carve up that caribou like he was slicing a peach.

I don't even like to clean a partridge.

In spite of the cold air, the smell of caribou innards make my stomach lurch. Ben pull the guts out onto the tundra, heaving his arms right into the middle of the dead animal, his sealskin mitts still on. I'm sorry to be so helpless but I can't think of a single thing to do except stand around freezing, wonder how soon I'm going to die. Ben clear the last of the guts out of the caribou.

"Crawl inside," he say to me, point down at the bloody cavity.

"Huh?"

"Crawl inside. Warm. Caribou will keep you alive."

"I can't," I say, gagging, and feeling faint at the idea.

"You'll be dead in less than an hour if you don't."

"What's the good? The caribou will freeze too."

"My brothers will come for us."

"How will they know?"

"They'll know."

"How will they know where we are?"

"They'll know. Now get inside," and Ben raise up his bloody mitt to me. I think he is about to hit me if I don't do as I'm told. All I can think of as I curl up like a not born baby, is what a mess I'll be – all the blood, and the smell.

"Face in," says Ben.

"Why?"

"You want your nose to freeze off?"

I squeeze into the cavity, breathe as shallow as I know how, my stomach in my throat, I'm scared as I've ever been. Ben drape the loose hide across my back. It *is* warm in there.

"Don't move. No matter what," he says. "My brothers will come. I'm going to the other animal. Don't move."

And I hear his first few steps on the ice and rock, then nothing. but the wind.

It pretty hard to guess how much time has passed when you freezing to death inside a dead caribou. I have a watch on, one of those $7.00 ones flash the time in scarlet letters when you press a button. But the watch is on my wrist, under my jacket and shirt, and I'm scared to make a move to look at it. I try thinking about some of the stories I still want to write, about my girl, Sadie One-wound, about some of the things I should of done in my life that I didn't. Still, time pass awful slow.

I'd guess maybe three hours. The more time go by, the more I know Ben has saved my life, even if it is temporary. Out in the open I'd be dead, and maybe Ben too, tough as he is.

Then from a long way away I hear the faint put-put-put of Skidoos. At first I'm afraid it is only the wind playing tricks, but the sound get louder, and finally a flash of light come through a crack between the ribs and the loose hide, hit the back wall of the caribou and reflect off my eye.

I try to move, but find I can't budge even an inch. I push and push. The caribou is froze stiff with me inside.

"Silas, Silas, you dead or alive or what?" I hear Frank yell.

"I'm here," I say. My voice sound to me like I'm yelling into a pillow.

There is a ripping sound as the hide pulled away from my back. Then Frank's hand shove a jug of walrus milk in front of my face, but I can't move to grab it and he can't position it so I can drink.

"Lie still." It is David Ammakar's voice. "We cut you out with a chain saw."

I hear the chain saw start. "Buzzzzz...rrrrr...zzz," go the saw. I know I ain't frozen when I can feel those blades about to cut into places all over my body. I sure hope Frank ain't operating it.

Eventually they cut the ribs away and somebody grab onto the back of my parka and pull me out onto the tundra.

Ben is there, smile his slow smile at me; his face is friendly, but his eyes is tough. We both look like we committed a mass murder.

"I told you they'd come," say Ben, slap the shoulders of his brothers with his big mitt. I tip up that jug of walrus milk, going down my throat it feel like kerosene that already been lit. But I don't mind. It great to be able to feel anything.

"Lucky they didn't leave the search up to me," says Frank. "Soon as we got home I borrowed five dollars from Andy Ammakar and was winning back my stake, when these guys, without even looking at a watch, all sit silent for a few seconds, listening, then Andy say, 'Ben ought to be back by now.' They get up, all three at the same time, right in the middle of a round, and head out to start their Skidoos."

"'Hey,' I said. 'Let's finish the game, and the walrus milk,' but they just get real serious expressions on their faces, and nobody say another word. We drive for miles through a snowstorm thick as milk, and find your Skidoo and you, first try. I don't know how these guys do it."

That night there is a celebration because me and Ben been brought back alive. An old man in a sealskin parka play the accordian. And we get served up food that I'm afraid to even think what it might be. A couple of men sing songs, unmusical, high-pitched chants, like the wind blowing over the tundra. A couple of other men tell stories about hunting.

Then Frank stand up and say, "Listen to me. I want to tell you a story of how I brought my brothers in from the cold." He then tell how he sensed we was in trouble, and how he convinced the Ammakar brothers to stop playing dice and drinking walrus milk, and start the search. When he is finished everyone laugh and pour Frank another drink.

"Come here," Ben Ammakar say to me. He carrying a funny little instrument, look something like a dulcimer, have only one string that I'd guess was animal and not metal. Ben pull at my arm.

"Why?" I say, holding back.

"You guys are here to learn about our culture. You and me going to sing a song to those two caribou, tell them how grateful we are that they saved our lives, ask them to forgive us for killing them before their time."

"I can't sing," I say.

"What kind of Indian are you?" say Ben. "When you open your mouth the song just come out, you don't have nothing to do with it." Ben pull me to my feet and we walk to the front of the little group.

He pluck at the dulcimer and it make a "plong, plong," sound, not musical at all. Ben sing a couple of flat notes, then make sounds in his throat like he imitating the call of some sad bird.

Frank staring around bold-faced, his black cowboy hat pushed to the back of his head. There are already two or three girls got their eyes bolted to him. "The best way to learn about any culture is to make love with their women," Frank said to me on the flight up. I bet he ain't gonna have to sleep alone for the rest of our stay here.

Ben Ammakar point at me and plonk on the dulcimer.

I've a truly flat voice and a tin ear. But it look like I've found a culture where everybody else have the same problem.

I've never felt so shy in front of a group of people. But I had a lot of time to think inside that dead caribou, and there no question it *did* save my life. I open my mouth and sing; the sound that come out is more high-pitched then I would of guessed, but flat as all the prairie. "Thank you Mr. Caribou for saving my life today. Please forgive me for killing you so I could go on living." After those first lines it is easy. Almost like when people get up and give testimonials at Pastor Orkin's church back home. Ben echoes my words, so do his brothers who sit in a circle on the floor in front of us. "Thank you Mr. Caribou for giving up your life," I sing, and as I do I raise the blood-stained arms of my parka towards the ceiling.

THE PERFORMANCE

This story came about because I read books. I read a book written by an Indian. One of the stories he told went a little like this: In maybe 1900 a bunch of Indians was at a big exhibition in St. Louis, which is down in the middle of the United States somewhere. They was hired to do a ceremonial dance, but they decide to dude-up that dance some, because at that exhibition was peoples from Africa who done really fierce dances. The Indians got to be friends with an African pygmy and he joined in their ceremony. They dressed up an Indian to look like a cannibal and right in the middle of that dance the cannibal make like he biting the pygmy and as he do blood spatter all over 'cause the Indians had killed a sheep beforehand. That pygmy disappear and all that's left on stage is blood and sheepmeat. There was thousands of people watch the dance, most believe what they see, send in police to arrest the cannibal. It was then the Indians perform a reverse dance, bring the pygmy back to life, leave the police and audience scratching their heads and saying "How did they do that?" while the Indians laugh behind their hands.

One rainy afternoon at Hobbema Pool Hall I tell my friends that story. We all have a good laugh on how they "put one over" on the white man, which is kind of what life is all about.

117

"I wonder if white men is still that dumb?" I say.

"I wonder if Indians is still that smart?" says Robert Coyote.

"You know," say Molly Thunder, who is just the best chicken-dancer in Western Canada, "we got a letter inviting us to perform at the Calgary Stampede in July."

By *us* Molly mean her and Carson Longhorn, my sister Delores, and the group of dancing students Molly teaches. The group call itself *The Duck Lake Massacre*, and come crashing on stage to the bang of drums and the whack of finger-cymbals. Molly's dancers is always decked out in feathered costumes and animal masks, look real scary. Audiences, even here on the reserve, always like to be scared just a little.

"Maybe you could liven up your show," says my friend Frank Fencepost. "I be your cannibal," and Frank bare his teeth, raise his arms over his head, jig around try to look fearsome.

"Sounds like fun," says Carson Longhorn, "but where would we get a pygmy?"

"They're little black midgets, aren't they?" says Molly.

That stop us all for a minute. Somebody suggest using a kid, but I bet even white people could tell the difference between a child and a pygmy.

Then a light shine over the heads of four or five of us at the same time.

"Melvin Bad Buffalo," we all yell. And we smile and slap each other on the shoulders.

Melvin Bad Buffalo is a genuine Indian dwarf. He at one time wrestled professionally. Wrestlers always have good guys and bad guys, and Melvin was a bad guy. I seen him wrestle once, when I was just a kid, at the Sales Pavilion in Edmonton. Rider Stonechild took me. Melvin come to the ring wear a black ten-gallon hat, a buffalo robe, and carry a spear. I remember that he bounced on the ropes a lot and was in a tag-team match partnered up with another Indian name of Little Beaver. They fought Tom Thumb and Pancho Villa, the Mexican Jumping Bean. Melvin Bad Buffalo pull the other wrestler's hair and gouge their eyes when the referee wasn't looking, which seem to be all the time.

After Rider brought me home, me and Frank and our friends play wrestling-match games for a month or two. But that was a lot of years ago and Melvin Bad Buffalo ain't fared so good. He is still a dwarf, got little tree-trunk legs, and a body solid as a ham. His head is normal size, tall and rectangular as a shoe-box. He ain't wrestled for a good five years I bet, and he just hang around the Alice Hotel, sweep the floor of the bar, empty ashtrays into a gallon tin what used to hold ketchup.

Melvin's real name is Crawford Piche, and he come from our reserve. Craw, as his old friends call him, have too much of a fondness for beer, and now got the start of a sad little belly, make him look like a starving kid.

He look at us like we was crazy when we ask if he like to join Molly's dance troupe.

"We gonna do a special dance at the Calgary Stampede and we need a pygmy. You figure you could act like one?"

"How much?" is all Crawford want to know. "They give us acting lessons at Wrestling School," he say with a crooked smile. "But I was made to promise I'd never tell."

"A hundred dollars every time we do the dance, and we supposed to do it three nights," say Molly Thunder. "That's more than anybody else is getting. And that's only if Mad Etta agrees to help us, and you mind your manners with the booze."

"That old walrus Etta couldn't cure somebody in perfect health," says Crawford Piche.

119

"A matter of opinion," I say.

"If she's so damn smart why couldn't she do nothin' for me?" he say, curl his big upper lip, take a crooked cigar out of a box in his shirt pocket and light it.

It true that Etta didn't do anything for Crawford, but it only because she didn't try, and the reason she didn't try was because he demanded a full cure and don't even say please.

"If I'm the only pygmy available I figure I should get $500 all told."

Him and Molly argue for a while, but he do have a point. Indian dwarfs is few and far apart. Molly finally give in.

Later on we tell Etta the story.

"You figure you can make that kind of magic?" I ask her.

"Do sows have tits?" says Etta. "Is Chief Tom snow-white inside?"

About the first of June the group have its first practice. That is when they find out what I always knew – that Frank Fencepost got at least three left feet, and no noticeable rhythm.

Molly Thunder is pretty smart though. It is my job to make Frank look like a cannibal. I got books out of the library and by rubbing on charcoal and then a little furniture wax, I make Frank black and shiny as a bowling ball.

To get a costume a couple of us climb up a pole at the Land of Eden Recreational Vehicle Center, outside Camrose, and we cut down a few of them triangular plastic flags that snap and crack in the wind. Frank going to wear a loincloth made from plastic flags.

"Loincloth got to come at least to my knee or my natural endowment frighten off the audience," Frank say, grinning. "Or else all the women will be rushing the stage." He stop for a minute. "Might not be such a bad idea at that."

When she find out Frank can't dance a lick, Molly Thunder take a chalk and draw two footprints on the stage, she then teach Frank to fit his own feet over the drawings. She have him stand like a weightlifter flexing his muscles, a calf-skull rattle in each hand.

"We're going to give you a permanent so you have fuzzy hair for the performance," Molly tell him. "All you have to do is bounce on one spot on the stage just like you were on a trampoline."

It is also my job to get Melvin Bad Buffalo ready for the dance. I call him Melvin to his face, 'cause I figure he like that better than his real name. I figure it best if I'm on the good side of anybody I got to rub down with charcoal and floor wax.

Still, Melvin usually show up for rehearsals hungover, unshaved, and as Frank say "Mean as a goat with a sore dick."

But when he want to Melvin can dance like hell and the program shape up real fast.

We into the second last week when Molly Thunder have Mad Etta come to rehearsals. By that time most everybody know their dance steps. All that is left is for Frank to attack Melvin Bad Buffalo, and for Etta to make that dwarf disappear in a splatter of blood.

Too bad Melvin Bad Buffalo is such a mean dude. First time Frank come up to him on stage, put his hands on Melvin, reach in as if he going to bite his neck, the professional wrestler in Melvin react. At least that's what Melvin said after he broke Frank's choke-hold and fling Frank over his shoulder. Frank get his wind knocked out and it about half an hour before he's ready to try again. He is about the palest-looking cannibal I ever seen.

Melvin throw Frank at least once on each of the first three

days they practise together.

"We ain't gonna need no phony blood," says Frank. "We just use Melvin's. I'll bite the head off him just like he was a chicken..."

"You're just the geek to do it," says Melvin.

They throw real punches at each other until we pull them apart. Frank come out on the short end of that fight too.

But if we thought we had problems with Frank and Melvin, they ain't nothing compared to what happen after Mad Etta arrive on the scene.

Etta's job is to sit the middle of the stage, on her tree-trunk chair, just like a queen, be decorated like a public Christmas tree, with furs and feathers and elk teeth. It take me and Rufus Firstrider a whole day to put super-strength casters on her chair so Etta can be wheeled around the stage. The dancers going to twirl and rattle all around her. There will be some cut-up meat hid under her costume. Frank and Melvin is to fight and while the dancers block off the audience view, Melvin Bad Buffalo going to be hid under Etta's dress, the dancers will run off stage wheeling Etta on her chair and all that will be left is Frank, all covered with blood, and a few pieces of meat people can believe used to be part of Melvin.

"We'll play it by ear after that," says Molly. "Audiences today are used to blood and guts on TV and in the movies; they may not give a care about what we done. If they don't make a fuss we don't do the second part of the dance."

Backstage on the first day Melvin say to Etta, "Listen you old elephant, let's get it straight that I'm only doing this for the money..."

"I thought I heard a voice," interrupt Etta, stare straight ahead over the top of Melvin's head. "Sound like that little polecat Crawford Piche. Anybody seen him around lately?"

Crawford-Melvin jump up and down to make himself seen.

"Oh, it *was* you talkin'," says Etta. "I thought maybe your mind might have growed up, even if the rest of you didn't. But I guess not. You was always dumb as a salt lick."

"You gonna get shot for a moose one day..."

Etta reach down and pick Melvin Bad Buffalo up by the biceps, lift him until they is face to face.

"It ain't nice to talk to your medicine lady in such a rude way. We going to work together. In fact you gonna be hid under my skirt..."

"If I knew that was part of the deal I never would of agreed. I'd rather be under a granary with seven skunks..."

"So if you want to live long and die happy," Etta go right on, "and have us use pig meat in the act instead of dead polecat, you better start being nice to know."

If Melvin's stare have heat to it, Etta would be fried golden. And though he don't talk back I bet he sure thinking rude thoughts.

We put on the show at Blue Quills Hall the last week of June, do everything but use the blood and pig meat. While Frank and Melvin act out their fight, all the dancers have their feathered bustles facing the audience, block off the view real good as Melvin get slipped under Etta's long, buckskin dress.

"Have to kill off a whole herd of moose just to cover that old woman," Melvin say, but never when Etta is within hearing.

When the dancers move aside there is Frank all alone, beat his chest like it was a drum, with Melvin nowhere in sight. The audience seem to like the dance.

So do the organizers at the Calgary Stampede who make us preview the act for them. They make everybody do that 'cause one time they got surprised by a stage act what have naked dancing in it. Seems people in Alberta aren't up to seeing anybody naked. Churches and newspapers kicked up a stink for months about that so now every act get looked at by representatives of the Stampede, a church minister, a school board member, and somebody from Alberta Culture, an organization that sometimes gives money to artists and writers as long as they promise to be unsuccessful. We don't even disappear Melvin at the Stampede preview.

"Look at the school-board lady," says Molly, "she likely to think there something nasty going on under Etta's skirts. Less these people know the better." And she's right, the school-board lady got a face like a dried apple and wear a green hat shaped like a sieve, have little wild roses growing out of it.

"Be nice to me, old woman," Melvin say to Etta before almost every practice, "I been known to play with matches," and he smile showing his bad teeth.

Melvin in his own way been sucking up to Mad Etta for the last couple of weeks, hoping I guess that she give him some medical attention. He bring her a bottle of beer a couple of times, and he give her a barrette for her hair, shaped like a butterfly. He claim he found it on the street, though my girl, Sadie, saw him buy it at the Woolco Store in Wetaskiwin. Can't say as I blame Melvin for wanting help, guess nobody likes being a dwarf. But he still act like it is something Etta owes him, just because he's there.

About two hours before we due to perform the dance for the first time, on the big outdoor stage at the Stampede, in front of 20,000 or more people, Melvin he go on strike.

"I want you to work some medicine on my body," he say to Etta, "or I ain't goin' on stage."

It hard for me to understand people like Melvin. Even

though he live his life in a white world, when the chips are down, he believe in the old ways and medicine.

"First," say Etta, sitting like a bear, way up on her tree-trunk chair, "it take me a week or more to prepare, and second, I never been able to change the way people was born. I can cure most sickness if the sick person believes in me..."

But Melvin don't let her finish. If he was just a good judge of character everything would of been okay. I can tell Etta is weakening, and she, in another minute, especially if the word *please* squeezed itself out of Melvin's mouth, would have agreed to at least try to cure him of some of his ills.

But Melvin Bad Buffalo don't see any of that. All he sees is a big, old woman tower over top of him, and he jump around like a kid who don't get his own way, call Etta every nasty name there is, plus two or three he invented himself.

When he finished swearing at Etta, Melvin decide to leave. But me and Frank and ten or so other people won't let him. He put up a certain amount of struggle, but we lock him in a box, big as a garbage dumpster, what used to hold everybody's costumes.

The time for the dance arrive. Rufus push Etta's chair on stage, while Etta hold Melvin by the shoulder, steer him along. Melvin look mean as any pygmy ever did.

The P.A. system announce the Duck Lake Massacre from Ermineskin Reserve, Hobbema, Alberta, and all the dancers rush on stage in a wave of color and a screech of sound. And the Mystical Dance of the Ermineskin Warrior Society be underway.

The drums throb loud and the dancers clatter around the stage, whirl, whirl, spin and swirl. Frank leap out, look so fierce he even scare me a little. Even Melvin Bad Buffalo dance like his pants was on fire.

The part of the circle at the front of the stage break open, now look a little like a horseshoe; Melvin and Frank circle each other, while above them, on her chair, Etta sit like a stone statue of a god.

Frank leap in and bite Melvin's neck; blood spurt ten feet in the air from the sausage skin Etta filled with something red and hid under Melvin's collar. The dancers stop running and rattling; they tiptoe around in their moccasins. The audience gasp when the blood splash, and the whole place get quiet.

Frank and Melvin finally lock together, Melvin scream a couple of times, and somebody in the audience answer him. The dancers close in around them, bustles toward the audience, rattles crackling like lightning.

I wheel Etta's chair off stage, pulling it straight back from where I been hid behind it. The dancers part again and there is Frank covered in more blood than most people care to see, chewing on a dripping piece of meat, that people might assume was part of Melvin Bad Buffalo, who, I hope, is comfortable and behaving himself under Etta's skirt.

The dancing stops. All the dancers including Frank take a bow. But it is plain to see the audience don't know whether to applaud or not.

"Half of them are in shock," says Etta, peering through a crack in the curtain.

One of the Stampede people who previewed our dance, has already arrived back stage, and is saying to anyone at all "What are you people trying to pull?"

The dancers all race off stage.

"I think we better do the second half of the dance," says Molly. "They fell for it."

The stage manager is tearing his hair. "You tricked us!" he yell at Molly. "There's no second half to your act."

"There is now," she says.

Suddenly there are about six blue-suited policemen back stage.

"We want to question the cannibal," says one of them.

Frank has put a blanket over his head and all that showing is his shiny black feet.

"Where's the little guy?" says another cop.

"We're going to bring him back to life right before your very eyes," says Molly. "Let's roll, guys," she yells, and the dancers all start quivering their rattles and thrumming their finger-cymbals.

The dancers charge onto the stage, all but running down the stage manager. I push Etta out.

"Where's the little squirt?" says Etta.

"I thought you had him," I say.

"Said he was going to the bathroom."

"Oh, oh," I say.

Frank dancing on his spot, waving pig meat in the air. He is supposed to slip the meat under Etta's chair, pull out Melvin Bad Buffalo. The dancers dance. They close up the circle. I push myself straight back until I'm off the stage. A policeman is soaking up blood with his handkerchief.

Melvin ain't nowhere to be seen. One of the cops has his gun drawn.

When Frank reach under Etta's skirt, he sure surprised to find nothing under there but Etta. The cops round us up, take us all to jail, tell us we stay there until they find Melvin alive and *in one piece*. Ever wonder how long it take to track down a dwarf in Calgary during Stampede Week?

THE BEAR WENT
OVER THE MOUNTAIN

"It ain't right that you get to prepare your stories in advance, Silas," my friend Frank Fencepost say to me. "I have to make mine up right there in the Welfare office."

Actually, my friends make more money from the Welfare each month than I make from all the books I had printed up, but having books printed up make me ineligible for Welfare. Somehow it don't seem fair. Only good thing is, I sometimes get invited to travel someplace to read my stories to an audience.

Just this week I got an invite to read at a college in Vancouver. They sent a letter say somebody called the Canada Council in Ottawa will pay me $200 and my air fare. All the reserves I know of have Tribal Councils, so I figure this Canada Council must be run by Indians. And probably rich Indians at that.

Boy, I never even guessed how much it cost to fly me from Edmonton to Vancouver and back. I went to two travel agencies in Wetaskiwin, two more in Edmonton, and then right to Air Canada itself, but they all want the same amount of money; exactly the same amount the college say they going to get the Canada Council to advance me.

"How much you figure it cost to drive to Vancouver and

back?" I ask Frank.

"Fred Muskrat drove there once and he said it took three tanks of gas each way. We'll take a little moose meat, and a .22 to hunt rabbits; we can make it a pretty cheap trip."

I already told Frank the college promise to put me up in a hotel and buy me food while I'm there.

"We'll take our girlfriends and make it a really good party," says Frank.

I kind of frown up my face.

"Hey, colleges is rich," says Frank. "They won't mind if you bring your friends along."

I figure that's true. But we really was just going to take our girlfriends: Sadie and Connie. But when we tell Mad Etta our medicine lady where we's off to, she stare at us real wistful and say, "You know, Silas, I always wanted just once to see the ocean before I die."

None of us ever seen the ocean. Me and Frank was to Las Vegas once; we seen Utah, Montana, and a couple of other states, but no ocean.

It pretty hard to turn down Mad Etta, not just 'cause she weigh 400 lbs. and might throw me through the screen door of her cabin if I make her cross, but because she look soulful when she ask.

Pretty soon me and Frank is loading Etta's tree-trunk chair in the back of Louis' pickup truck, and rigging up a canvas to keep the wind off her as we driving over the mountains. Etta's all decked up in a bear-skin coat make her look pretty large. "If we was to plant a few trees on her, a whole troop of boy scouts could go hiking," whisper Frank.

When they learn about the trip, lots of our friends, and especially my littlest sister Delores, want to come with us. But we say no to everybody.

The money from the Canada Council arrive, just like the

man in Vancouver, a Professor George Something-or-other from Simon Fraser University, say it would. Professor George say he writes books, too, but I never heard of him. We got a guy called Simon Fraser live right here on the Ermineskin Reserve; he sure is surprised to learn he got a university named for him. We can't very well say no when *he* ask to come along, and if we taking our girlfriends, no reason why he shouldn't take his.

Simon Fraser is short and wide, wear a 10-gallon black-felt hat, and a wide belt with a turquoise buckle. His girl is Lucy Three Hand. Lucy ride the rodeo circuit and is one of the best lady cowboys on all the Prairies. She is pretty, too; slim, with skin the color of floor wax, and always wear a scarlet bandana tied in her hair. She is a champion calf-roper and carry along her coil of rope.

Then Mr. and Mrs. Blind Louis Coyote decide to come, too. Louis he own the truck, and he ain't never seen the ocean neither. Mrs. Blind Louis figure if she was to duck Louis' head in the ocean water it might bring back his eyesight. They dress up in their mackinaws and climb under Etta's canvas, even though we offered to let them ride in the cab.

The first part of the trip through Calgary and Banff ain't so bad, but then the mountains get higher and even in low gear Louis' old truck groan and puff something awful getting up them long hills. But it roll down the other side pretty easy. The brakes ain't working so good, but the truck's always stopped before. Although it ain't always had Mad Etta in the back on a downhill grade.

Near this town called Revelstoke there is a hill about 10 miles long. About halfway down, when I touch the brake my foot go straight to the floor. At about the same time Frank point out that behind us is an RCMP car got his flasher turning.

As we traveled we was singing that old song about the bear went over the mountain, you probably heard it:

The bear went over the mountain
The bear went over the mountain
The bear went over the mountain
To see what he could see

But all that he could see
Was the other side of the mountain
The other side of the mountain
The other side of the mountain
Was all that he could see.

Instead of slowing down we picking up speed, and I swear the flashing light on the RCMP car look mad. The girls is still singing but in pretty small voices, 'cause they holding on real tight.

We go faster and faster. As we come around a curve I can see the town down in the valley, look as if I'm seeing it from an airplane. Somebody in the back is slapping on the roof of the cab. I see a sign say *Runaway Truck Exit One-Quarter Mile*. It make me glad I can read.

Only trouble is that between me and that exit road is a flat-bed truck got a Caterpillar riding on it, go only about 40 mph. There is a whole string of traffic coming *up* the hill toward us. If I was one of them Dukes of Hazzard I'd jump my truck right over the flat-bed, or drive under it, but real life ain't like that. I head into the oncoming traffic and hope they is smart enough to pull over.

We skin around the truck, even lose the RCMP what been driving like he was glued to our bumper. A sports car coming toward us miss us by about a foot, make a buzzing sound as it pass, like a bumblebee going by my ear.

But our troubles ain't over yet. Sometime while we was

131

passing the flat-bed we miss the runaway-truck exit.

"Pastor Orkin, where are you now that we need you?" yells Frank.

We going 85 mph and picking up speed. I guess the only thing that save us is Louis' truck so old it can't go no faster. Even though we go around a corner on two wheels, and I see Etta's tarpaulin come loose and it flap like a parachute above us, I manage to keep the truck right side up until I see a service station at the bottom of the hill. The entrance is on an upgrade, but not enough...

We shoot through the air for about 40 feet, land with a crash and head for a gravel pit, that I can see is full of water. At the last second I cut the wheels and we swing in a wide arc, spray gravel all across the front of the service station, break the window like it was machine-gunned.

I look at Sadie, Connie and Frank. We is all pretty pale.

"Were you scared?" I say to Sadie, who still clinging to my arm.

"Only thing I worry about," says Frank, "is I heard once you could turn white from fear."

The RCMP is sitting right on my bumper. I get out of the truck, my knees wobbly as a day-old calf. I see my littlest sister Delores was in the truck-box after all. I guess she hid behind Etta's chair, or just behind Etta.

"That was fun, Silas," she says with a big, missing-toothed smile. "Let's do it again."

"You're under arrest," say the RCMP.

"We sure do want to thank you for guiding us down the hills there," says Frank real innocent. "Ain't every officer who would be able to see we was in trouble..."

That constable look around to be sure it is him Frank is talking to. Frank heard a line on the TV one night: "You never get a second chance to make a first impression," and he been practising it every chance he get.

The constable has pink cheeks and a fuzzy brown must-ache, look like it made of weatherstripping. After he check and find we really had no brakes, he decide to let us go. "I'm gonna call the Game Warden, though," he say. "I don't think you're allowed to carry a bear in the truck-box without a muzzle."

"Tame bear," says Frank.

"My little sister's pet," I say. "Smarter than the average bear, too."

"This here's Simon Fraser," says Frank. "Got a university named for him."

"Grrrrr," says Etta from under the tarpaulin.

It take most of our money to get the brakes fixed, but the rest of the trip go pretty smooth.

First place we go in Vancouver is the hotel where the university supposed to have bought me a room. I seen a hotel like that in Las Vegas one time: mirrors all over the place – people who live in hotels sure must like to look at themselves – carpets soft as muskeg and snooty people everywhere, with oiled hair and frozen smiles.

"Snotty Towers," says Frank.

Turn out we is three days early for my reservation, which is only for one night anyway.

"How about if we stay tonight?" I say. "We worry about three days from now when it get here."

The lady desk clerk have on a pink jacket, her hair is blond, and she could be pasted right to a magazine cover she look so pretty.

"Who is *we*?" she ask, giving me a fishy eye. "The reservation is for a Mr. Silas Ermineskin. One person, one single room."

"Right," I say. "I'll just send my family here down to skid row, soon as I let them have a look at the room."

"I don't think that will be possible, Mr. Ermineskin."

And I guess that she is about to call in reinforcements, when Frank push himself up close to the counter.

"Boy, I bet there's some roses someplace fistfighting to see if they can smell as good as you," Frank say, and stare right into the eyes of that girl in the pink jacket.

I expect her to tell Frank not to be so smart, but she don't. Instead she stare him back fish-eyed for half a minute or more before she break into a big smile.

"Thanks," she say. "I bet there are two garbage cans someplace fighting to see which one can smell most like you," but even though she tries she can't say that in a nasty way.

"What time do you get off work?" ask Frank. And that girl tell him.

"You just drop up to my friend's room. If I ain't in make yourself at home. It'll be worth the wait."

Behind us Frank's girl, Connie, got her hands on her hips. "How you figure I'll look with that blond wig on my belt?" she ask.

"I don't think that's a wig," I say.

"Not yet," say Connie.

Frank turn around to her and whisper. "Hey, I'm just doin' a good deed. I'm gonna sacrifice my body so we all have a place to stay." And he put a finger to Connie's pouting lip.

"If I catch you together you both gonna have dimes on your eyes," say Connie.

About this time Mad Etta come waddling through the double doors.

"I'm growing moss on my north side from being out there in the rain," she says. "What's takin' you so long?"

The pink lady give me the key.

Boy, do we have a nice time. I learned how to use this here room service when me and Frank was in Las Vegas. We have them send up drinks, and then we all go to the dining room for supper. Delores have a red-colored drink called a Shirley Temple, which I guess must be named for a church of some kind, and all the chocolate sundaes she can eat; they bring the sundaes to her on a silver dish so tall she have to kneel on her chair just to get at it.

Frank borrow $20 from the girl on the desk, give it to Connie so she can go shopping. And while the rest of us eat, Frank rests in my room with the blond-haired girl.

In the morning the desk clerk, who by now is a man, but smell just as good as the lady, is worried about all the charges we made. When Frank discover he could make long-distance phone calls, he spend a certain amount of money trying to reach Morgan Fairchild. He knows if he could just talk to Morgan Fairchild he could get a date. "I just describe to her how I come to be named Fencepost and she send me a ticket for the next plane to California."

"Don't worry," I tell the clerk. "This is all paid for by Simon Fraser University. And this guy over here *is* Simon Fraser." Simon take off his black hat and bow to the clerk.

Out on the street it is warm but pouring rain. We head to the Indian part of town, but we forgot it was Sunday and there ain't no bars open so we got no place to meet any friends. Seem to me Vancouver ain't much different than Edmonton or Calgary. Somehow I thought people wouldn't be so poor where the weather was nice. And that people would feel better about themselves where the country was warm and beautiful. But there's more winos and street people than I ever seen anywhere.

"I want to walk in the ocean," says Mad Etta. And so does Delores. Mrs. Blind Louis still want to dip Louis' head in the salt water.

"Where's there a good beach?" we ask an Indian man lean on a parking meter on East Hastings Street.

"What you want is Wreck Beach," he say after a long pause. "Here tell they got nude bathers down there."

"I'm all for that," says Frank, jump up and down some.

"I show you where it is if I can come along for the ride," says the fellow, who take about a full minute just to say that sentence.

"You stuck on 33 rpm or what?" says Frank.

The fellow just smile; he do that slow, too, and tell us his name is Bobby Billy, and he come from a place sound like Sasquash.

"So how do you Flat-face Indians like Vancouver?" Frank ask Bobby Billy as we drive along.

"We don't like being called Flat-face Indians," say Bobby Billy. "I'm a Squamish Indian, come from up in the mountains there," wave toward the big peaks look down on the city.

"Hey, I don't mean no offence," says Frank. "It okay if you want to call us Big-tall-handsome Indians. We don't mind."

Bobby Billy's face break into another slow smile and I see we going to be friends. He have me drive through the grounds of "The University," which I guess to be Simon Fraser. We drive a road that goes right through the middle of a golf course, and then we park where we can see the ocean for a long ways, just like it was prairie.

We get out and Bobby Billy stare at our licence plates for a long time before he say real slow, "I hear the government here in B.C. give all the bum drivers yellow licence plates," and he try to keep his face serious.

Some people are already making their way down a winding trail to the beach.

"If you go down there, how are we gonna get you back up?" Frank ask Etta."

"You let Etta worry about that," she say. "I'm not gonna get this close and not dip myself in the ocean."

"Raise the water level by five feet," says Frank, but quietly.

The sun has come out and the ocean waves look like they full of sequins. There is lots of people on the beach and in the water, and just like Bobby Billy said, off at one end is a section where people have no clothes on. We are the only people there who ain't white.

"First Indians should have had stricter immigration laws," says Bobby Billy.

Frank go clomping right over to the nude section of the beach, although he wearing lumberjack boots, jeans, a couple of shirts, a mackinaw, and a cowboy hat with a green feather stick up over the top.

"Smells like bad fish," says Blind Louis, facing into the breeze, his nostrils spread wide as he take in the air.

"We gonna dip your head in the water, find out if it make you see again or not," says Mrs. Blind Louis.

Mad Etta has waddled over to the naked side of the beach, carrying her tree-trunk chair; she set the chair down and it look from where I am as if she taking off her five-flour-sack dress.

"I don't know what everybody so excited about," says Connie. "Everybody is always naked under their clothes."

Then she draw in her breath. "Look at that!" she say, point at a man who is even more natural than everybody else. "Wow! Paint it silver and you got yourself a hell of a flashlight," says Connie.

Lucy Three Hand, the lady cowboy, has brought her rope and is practising throw lassos over Simon Fraser.

"I wish I could go in the water," says Delores, "but I don't have a bathing suit."

"You could go down to the far end of the beach there, where people have no clothes on," I say. But Delores look at me like I just broke her favorite doll, sniff up her nose just like she was a Christian, let me know in language I didn't even know she knew, that she is "grossed out" by naked people.

Frank run down the beach like he was an animal of some kind, let Lucy Three Hand rope him. Quite a crowd gather around to watch. The water has worked its way up to Mad Etta, and she sitting down on the sand, let the water splash over her big brown toes.

Sadie and me walk back up the path, holding hands. For quite a while we walk around the university, look at the big buildings, try to guess which one I might do my reading in. Me and Sadie enjoy the sunshine and soft grass, kiss each other some. I think I agree with Bobby Billy, who say on the way out here, "Weather in Vancouver's so good, only way the old-timers could start a graveyard was to kill somebody."

But when we get back halfway down the hill where we can see the beach, it look as if a riot taking place. All the Indians is gathered in a circle and surrounded by white people.

"That sure ain't the way it's done in the movies," I say to Sadie as we pick our way down the trail. Some dudes in their altogether is holding Frank in the air. Everyone is yelling.

"Keep your filthy hands off our women," one of the men say.

"I got *invited* to touch," Frank is saying while he kick the air.

Mad Etta is wet all over, her hair slicked down like it been oiled. She is pointing her fist at a group of men in green shirts, who are trying to say something to her – apologizing, I think – but she ain't listening very closely.

Bobby Billy and Simon Fraser stand off to one side, Bobby smile kind of secret as if he know something we don't.

Lucy Three Hand twirl her rope in a circle, while the yelling just keep getting louder and louder.

It is then that a policeman come along. At least he wear a uniform and carry a gun. I can't figure if he's RCMP, a Park Warden, or only one of them Commissionaires, who are mostly old army guys who like to have a job where they can push people around.

The policeman sure don't have any trouble making up his mind about who is wrong.

"You're under arrest," he say to Frank.

"Like hell," yells Connie. "He wasn't doin' nothin'."

"You too, sister," says the cop.

At this time Mad Etta pick up one of the green-shirted men and toss him into the ocean.

"What's happened?" I say to Bobby Billy.

Bobby take about 30 seconds before he answer me and another 30 seconds to speak his sentence: "Those men are from the Greenpeace Ship, spend all their time saving whales. They took poles and try to roll yonder big lady into the ocean."

At least I understand why Etta is angry.

"See how you like it," Etta is saying.

"Assault Causing Bodily Harm," says the uniform, point at Etta. "I'm taking you into custody, sir."

Etta pick up another greenshirt and heave him at the cop, who just manage to duck. I bump the constable's arm and his gun fire into the air.

All of a sudden that uniform got his gun pointed right at my nose.

"Disturbing the Peace, Assaulting a Police Officer," he say at me.

I can smell the hot barrel of the gun. Then it ain't there anymore, 'cause Lucy Three Hand roped the constable, and his hands is tight to his sides as if he standing in a broom closet.

"Back off!" Frank yell at the white people. "Boo!" And they back up a step or two. The green-shirted men all run off carrying their poles. Sadie collect Mr. and Mrs. Blind Louis from where they been in the ocean.

"Just because I'm blind don't mean my eyes can't feel," Louis is saying.

"If it don't hurt, it don't do you no good. You'll probably be able to see tomorrow," say Mrs. Blind Louis.

Lucy got the constable trussed up like a pig, and someone else taken his gun and tossed it in the ocean. But I notice he talking into the walkie-talkie in his shirt pocket, more screaming than talking.

We all head up the trail to the cliff-top, three or four of us pushing on Etta's back. Turn out when Etta is angry she can climb hills pretty good.

It is while we loading up the truck that about 10 cars surround us: RCMP, Park Wardens, University Security, and a truck from Customs and Immigration.

We all get arrested, but me, Frank, and Mad Etta more than anybody else.

"At least we don't have to worry about how we going to pay for a hotel," says Mad Etta, wring salt water out of the skirt of her five-flour-sack dress, in the back of the police van.

In court the next afternoon, the police, some lawyers and a judge have a meeting for about 10 minutes at the front of the courtroom.

The judge stare over at Etta a couple of times. "They really thought she was beached?" I hear him say. The judge tell us if we promise to head right back to Alberta he dismiss all charges.

We promise.

"I'm sorry I keep such bad company, your honor," say Bobby Billy. "I never hang around with Alberta Indians again. From now on I just associate with regular murderers and thieves."

"See that you do," says the judge.

It take us the rest of that day and part of the next to find Delores, who because she was a kid, was kind of repossessed by some social workers. They took her to Victoria for some reason and we had to wait around while they found her and flew her back.

"I got to eat in a restaurant, and ride on a ferry, and fly in an airplane that land on the water, and they bought me a doll..." Delores say in a rush when she first see us. Delores, I guess, wasn't half as worried about us as we was about her.

After we get Delores back I realize I'm a day or two late for the reading I was supposed to do. We first go to the wrong university; I never even thought there could be two universities in the same city. It take us a couple of hours just to find Simon Fraser University, and even then I have to park the truck on a lawn because all the parking lots is full.

"You were supposed to be here last night," that Professor George yell at me, when I finally find his office.

"I can read today; it don't make no difference to me."

"There were 180 people here last night and you didn't show up."

I don't think Professor George would want to know the real reasons, so I just tell him I'm late because I still think in Indian time. "I don't know what you're so upset about," I say. "I got here within a couple of days of when I was supposed to," and I smile real innocent.

"You won't get paid unless you do a reading; not that you

deserve to," says Professor George, "but I'll arrange for you to read in the Faculty Lounge at noon."

I read a story to 20 or so professors, shabby-looking men with piercing eyes. Most of them could pass for winos at a Salvation Army meeting. I heard once that a story writer got to be dead before they find out who you are at a university. Guess that's true, 'cause these guys don't laugh where they supposed to, and is more interested in staring at Mad Etta and Lucy Three Hand than in hearing me.

On the way home Mad Etta pull a soggy $50 bill from her moccasin so we don't have to play gas-and-run at a service station. We buy some Cheezies and Fritos and ice-cream bars and somebody start singing "The Bear Went Over the Mountain."

"Smart bear would of stayed home," says Etta. And I have to agree.

DANCING

Pastor Orkin from the Three Seeds of the Spirit, Predestinarian, Bittern Lake Baptist Church, sure been getting himself and his church a lot of publicity lately. Come Saturday night there going to be a big burning at the church grounds: records, books, newspapers, magazines, tapes, even some clothes that the church don't agree with.

On the front page of this week's *Wetaskiwin Times* is a picture of Pastor Orkin all dressed up in his white church dress, his arms raised up over his head, with a big fire burning behind him. The picture was from a wiener roast the church held a year or two ago, but it go pretty good with the headline which read: LOCAL CHURCH TO BURN ACCOUTREMENTS OF EVIL.

Me and my friend Frank Fencepost, and our girlfriends was at that wiener roast. For us Indians, what religion we is, depend on who is holding the church picnic. Me and Frank and Connie and Sadie and sometimes quite a few of our friends been to every church-sponsored pot-luck supper, pancake feed, or beef barbecue within sixty miles, ever since I been old enough to drive Louis Coyote's pickup truck. In return for free food we is willing to put up with whatever these church people got to throw at us.

Pastor Orkin at first used to run something called the Wayside Fundamental Baptist Church of the Fourth Dimension. He only had about six people who followed him and they didn't even have a church but used to meet in the Sons of Sweden Community Hall over near Camrose. In those days Pastor Orkin work in the accounts payable department of the John Deere Tractor Store in Wetaskiwin. Then he hook up with a couple of little old ladies who build the Three Seeds of the Spirit Church. They build it with money their dead brother earned from bootlegging, but they never know that. At first the old ladies hold their services in the morning, while Pastor Orkin have his in the afternoon. Now, them old ladies is in a nursing home in Wetaskiwin. I guess they give their church to Pastor Orkin.

Of all the religious people we come in contact with; they mostly all make a try at converting us Indians at one time or another, these fundamentalists is the strangest. "I think we just don't know it," say Frank, "but I bet the churches get paid a bounty for every Indian they convert. Instead of our ears they send in a form to the government and collect a dollar or so. Why else would they be after us the way they are?"

A lot of the time I think Frank is right. What is strange about these fundamentalists is that they *don't* want us. "God is hate," is how Frank describe what Pastor Orkin preach. And he preach it longer and louder and wilder than any of the other churches. He hate Indians, Catholics, Jews, all foreigners, and everybody who don't believe exactly like he does.

We check to be sure there going to be good food before we go near Pastor Orkin. Funny thing is that the mean-looking little women with red hands and bony knuckles, is the best cooks around.

"Would you be a better cook if we gave up sex?" ask Frank. We all laugh at that, 'cause Connie can't even burn water.

One time somebody at her house won a pound of coffee. Connie'd never seen anything but instant coffee in her life, so she just put a spoon of the real coffee in a cup and poured hot water on it.

"Tasted like mud-pie coffee we used to cook up when we was little kids," says Frank.

"Which would you rather have, good biscuits or good lovin'?" ask Connie.

Frank grin. "I'll steal the biscuits; you just stay fat and sexy."

Pastor Orkin and his church really *don't* want us as members. They claim we going to hell because our skin is dark. That should make us stay away, but it don't. Pastor Orkin and his followers is kind of like little kids trying to act bad by saying dirty words. No matter what they say, it comes off sounding foolish.

And it makes us feel good when we give them trouble.

"Hey, Pastor Orkin," Frank say, "you figure people with sun tans going to hell like us Indians? I mean they got dark skin just like us."

"Of course not," says Pastor Orkin.

"But how can you tell the difference between a white man with a dark sun tan and a pale Indian? Aren't you afraid you'll make a mistake?"

"The Lord knows the difference. The Lord is all-seeing."

"Yeah, but how can *you* tell which is which? I mean if I was locked up in a church for a year or two, I might get as white as you. Then wouldn't you feel bad for not lettin' me join your church?"

Frank give Pastor Orkin a bad time every time we visit their church. Their ads in the *Wetaskiwin Times* and the *Camrose Canadian* always say *everybody welcome*. Bet they'd really like to add *No Indians*, but there may even be a law against them doing that.

"Why do you insist on turning up where you're not welcome!" Pastor Orkin yell at Frank one Sunday.

"My stomach can't tell if the strawberry shortcake is Catholic, Lutheran, or Four Square," says Frank.

Frank he figure we should start our own religion.

"We could steal a few chairs, put them in that empty storefront by the Alice Hotel. We'd put up a sign say Church of the Holy Fencepost. I'd get me a white sheet to wear, and I'd just stand around with my arms raised saying, 'Bless this here Fencepost.' Silas, you could read from the Bible, and Connie and Sadie could sing 'I Saw the Light,' and Robert Coyote and Eathen Firstrider would take up the collection and slap everybody on the side of the head who didn't give at least five dollars."

We first hear about the burning over the radio. We always listen to CFCW 'cause it play all country music; bad thing is they play too many hymns, and in the evenings there is evangelists who beller for an hour or two at a time. They also let local ministers talk late at night and that was where we heard Pastor Orkin.

"Tell us again why you're going to burn all these things, Pastor Orkin," say the announcer.

"There is enough temptation in the world without young people being exposed in such a direct manner as by listening to Rock music, or dancing. And believe me dancing is temptation. A dancing foot and a praying knee do not belong on the same leg," yell Pastor Orkin.

I've always wondered if a lot of people who go to church are deaf. If that is why most ministers yell. Or if the people is deaf because most ministers yell.

That statement about the foot and the knee is the funniest

thing we heard for a long time.

"I wonder if it's alright to have a praying foot and a dancing knee," says Connie Bigcharles, and we all laugh until we got tears in our eyes. But listening to Pastor Orkin is scary too, 'cause these religious peoples is never satisfied just to follow what they believe; they want to force their ways on everyone. It strange how something can make you angry, but make you laugh at the same time.

Late Friday night, after we been in town for a movie, we drive past Pastor Orkin's church. *The Church of the Open Heart* is what the sign say across the top of the double doors. But underneath there is a padlock the size and thickness of a slice of black bread.

Outside in the yard is a round-topped signboard list the hours for services and stuff. Also behind that glass is a photograph of Pastor Orkin flashing his big, wide, store-bought teeth, and with his store-bought hair falling over his forehead. When we first knew Pastor Orkin he was almost bald and had pointy teeth with black spots on them.

"Why didn't you just pray for new hair and fat teeth, instead of spending money on them?" Frank ask him one time. Pastor Orkin sure didn't like that 'cause there were a lot of people standing around after the service.

Frank take a look at that padlock.

"Want to go inside?" he ask. "Hell, I could open this lock with my dick."

We nod our heads, and it take Frank all of ten seconds to spring the lock.

Inside, the main floor is just like most churches, a few rows of blond-wood benches, a red carpet down the middle aisle, an altar, flags, mirrors, stained glass, and crosses all over the place.

The basement is just like Blue Quills Hall on the reserve – a polished hardwood floor with basketball, volleyball, and badminton courts drawn on it. There is a stage with toys scattered all over, and some blue velvet curtains partway closed, with little kids' drawings pinned on. The place smell of varnish, running shoes and wet mittens.

It is a few minutes before we see that the stuff to be burned is behind the closed part of the curtain. It heaped up to six feet high in some spots: books, records, tapes, clothes, toys, sports equipment.

"I wonder how come these holy people own so much evil stuff?" says Frank.

On shelves at the back of the stage is the church's own collection of records and books. They also got a tape deck and an expensive stereo set.

"Let's put on a record and I'll dance," says Connie. "If Pastor Orkin is right, I'll be struck by lightning and the rest of you can convert. I'm willing to take the chance," and she sway back and forth some, wiggle the toes of her cowboy boots.

"No. This is their place," I hear myself saying. "Even if what they believe is crazy, they got rights."

Connie wrinkle her nose at me and Frank make a rude noise, but they don't turn on the record player.

"Look at this book," call out Sadie. "It's called *Birth Control Through Prayer*."

"All you got to do is hold that book between your knees and you'll never get pregnant," says Frank.

There must be over 500 record albums on shelves along the back wall, most of them hymns, sung by choirs and quartets, and lone people, all of them white, and all resembling the people who attend the church. There is one whole shelf of records that is nothing but sermons by beefy looking preachers, wear blue suits and have lots of oiled-up hair.

"Look at the people on this record jacket," says Frank, "long dresses, no make-up, all scowling..."

"And those are just the men," says Connie.

"Hey, Silas," yells Frank. "You know why Pastor Orkin and his friends never have sex standing up?"

"No, I don't know, and I probably don't want to," I say.

"Boy, look at all this stuff they're gonna burn," says Sadie. "Here's a Willie Nelson record, and a Merle Haggard, and a Dolly Parton..."

"And here's a tape by *Abba*," say Connie, "and one by *Kiss*, and here's the *Beatles*..."

"Here's one by Johnny Cash. I thought he was religious..."

"Not enough, I guess."

"Let's carry off as much as we can," says Frank. "We can sell what we don't use." But me and Sadie say no.

"It is *their* stuff," we argue. "They should be able to do what they want."

"But look at this sweater," says Connie. "I bet it cost fifty dollars. It's a real crime to burn it."

"I guess it would be okay to exchange," I say, "as long as you leave yours."

Connie and Frank have their clothes changed in about a minute. I even exchange my running shoes. I sure wonder why they was gonna burn the ones I'm wearing now.

Just as Frank's about to lock up the door, I notice one of my new shoelaces is about worn through.

"I'll be right back," I say to my friends, run into the church and down the stairs into the basement.

Come Saturday night, a truckload of us drive up to the Three Seeds of the Spirit, Predestinarian, Bittern Lake Baptist Church, to see the goings on. We ain't the only curious ones. I bet all of the church's one hundred or so members is there, and so is a TV crew from Edmonton, a lot of newspaper and radio people, and a couple of hundred folks from around Wetaskiwin, Camrose, and even Edmonton, all come to see the burning.

There is a young guy, 17 or 18, got a long, straight face like a horse, is standing by the big pile of stuff to be burned. A lady TV reporter pick up one of the record albums and stare at the cover.

"This is a Lawrence Welk album," she say to the young guy, who have his hair brushcut, and wear a white shirt, tie and jacket. "What could you possibly find offensive about Lawrence Welk?"

"Must be that he plays *champagne music*," calls out Connie.

"Well, ma'am," that young fellow say, "it's just that that kind of music is conducive to dancing, and dancing sort of reminds us of sex..." and he pause for a long time.

"I can never figure out why these church people got so much against sex," says Connie. "It's fun and it's free and there ain't no tax on it."

"What I can't figure is how these types ever get any kids," says Frank.

"I bet they order them up from the Sears catalogue," says Connie.

"They just phone the stork and put in an order for a religious baby," says Frank.

"One of these books is a *cookbook*," says the TV lady. "How do you explain that?"

"They use wine in some of the recipes," the boy reply, and there ain't even a flicker of a smile on his face.

Religious peoples and people who get elected to their jobs always take the world deadly serious. They never guess that by being so serious they make most people laugh at them.

"How can you deny music?" the TV lady go on. "It's like denying the birds, or the wind. Do bird songs remind you of sex?"

I bet that boy wishing Pastor Orkin would rescue him, but the pastor know when to make himself scarce.

"Yeah, how about the wind?" says Connie. "Careful or it'll blow in your ear and get you all excited."

"What are *those*?" the TV lady say, pointing to a couple of big cartons that stuffed to bursting with clothes.

"Satan's apparel," say the boy, again with a straight face.

The reporter picks up a few of the pieces. "These are just blue jeans, and sweaters, and shorts, and a bathing suit."

"They cause prurient thoughts," says the boy.

"What's that?" says Connie, sticking her face in so she's sure to be on TV.

"Unclean thoughts. Sexual thoughts."

"I thought clothes was supposed to," says Connie, smirking at the boy and wiggling her hips. Connie's jeans is so tight Frank claim he can count her pussy hairs through the denim.

The boy stare at Connie and get all red; he swallow hard, his adam's apple running up his throat like a golf ball.

A while later the fire bloom up in the night sky, the flickering flames make people's eyes flash red. Each member of the Three Seeds of the Spirit church take a turn carrying some books or records or tapes up to the fire. Some of them are farmers wearing suits too short in the sleeves and legs, or farm ladies in dull dresses or baggy pant-suits, the real ugly kind like the Queen wears. But mostly they is young people: boys who ain't used to wearing suits, and pale girls in plain, ankle-length dresses, their long hair reflecting the firelight.

These people sure wouldn't like it if anyone suggested they was dancing. But they are. Sure as they been born with rhythm in their bodies.

Pastor Orkin arrive in his church dress. He stand on the church steps and pray some, but in a voice can be heard a mile away. He only allow each person to carry one object on each trip to the fire. The pastor know that when you got a good thing going you make it last as long as possible.

"Brother Sylvester," he call to the horse-faced boy, "bring the record player out here. We will play some joyful music and sing our praises for a job well done."

There is already a record on the turntable when brother Sylvester, carrying an armful of albums, wrestle the record player into place, trailing a long orange extension cord. Pastor Orkin turn up the volume, and what they call joyful music blast out into the night. The church people walk, trot, even run up to the fire, all to the beat of that music; they feel the pulse of it, the vibration.

Pastor Orkin carry some of the last records toward the fire; he spin them into the flames like frisbees, smiling his biggest and most self-satisfied smile.

"There goes Willie Nelson," call Connie, and all of us clap our hands right along with the church people.

As they getting ready to start burning the clothes and sports equipment, Pastor Orkin change the music. He take a record out of the jacket for *Great Hymns of the Western World*. But when he set down the needle what come out is an outlaw country singer name of Johnny Paycheck singing a song called "Take this Job and Shove it!" Pastor Orkin rip the needle off the record, stare around more wild-eyed than usual, then bound up the steps like a big dog and disappear into the church.

A few seconds later, from deep in the church we can hear him howl like the devil just kicked him in the shins. On the steps, brother Sylvester is taking records from their jackets, reading the labels in the firelight and not looking happy.

Frank stare at me for a long time before his face break into a big smile, as he realize that he ain't the only one capable of playing a trick now and then.

REAL INDIANS

I knew Hogarth Running Eagle when he was just plain Martin Johnson, who got kicked out of the Tech School in Wetaskiwin for carting off 49 slide rules and two dozen pocket calculators and selling them from a divider at the parking lot of the Wheatlands Shopping Center in Camrose.

"Hell, I figured pocket calculators was supposed to go in your pocket," and he grin wide and friendly, his eyes narrowing as if a light shining in them. "And them slide rules slid right along after me as I was leaving the building."

Martin worked on a combining crew for a month, earn over $900, buy himself two expensive suits, a blue one and a black one, some white-on-white shirts, and he let the clothing salesman pick out his ties for him.

"Back when I was ignorant, it was hard to tell the difference between quality and color. See, I would have picked bright ties – yellows, reds, greens; I had my eye on a pink one," and he smile that thousand dollar smile of his again. "See when I went to apply for a job as a car salesman, the sales manager said, 'I like the way you're dressed, understated, expensive but not garish. Most Indians would buy a $300 suit and then stick a $10 piece of plastic Indian jewelry around his neck.'

"'I'm not an ordinary Indian,' I told him."

And he wasn't either.

"I'm an entrepreneur now," say Hogarth Running Eagle.

"What? You changed tribes? You ain't a Cree no more?" say Frank.

"No. I'm a businessman, but a special kind with a whole lot of irons in the fire."

He sell cars like the word no wasn't one he knew the meaning of. It was while he was selling cars that he changed his name.

"It gave me an advantage. You got to take every advantage you can get. I mean, Martin Johnson doesn't have any class. When I told customers my name was Hogarth Running Eagle, they had new respect for me. They trusted me. I mean, if you can't trust a poor, downtrodden, native Indian to sell you a good car, who can you trust?" and he smile crooked, showing how his teeth been capped.

While he was selling cars he started managing an Indian Rock band called *Redcrow*, and they got to be well known at least at the Royal Hotel Bar in Edmonton.

Since then he's sold water softeners, roofing materials, and have a crew of guys hawking discount coupons for restaurants give two meals for the price of one.

Then somehow he get interested in the travel business.

"I just said to myself one day after I seen all those ads in the window of a travel agency for Europe, Asia, Hawaii, the Bahamas, 'I bet people from far away would be interested in seeing Indian Reserves.'"

His company is called Reservation Enterprises Ltd. "We Take Reservations to See Reservations," is his slogan.

I think maybe Hogarth Running Eagle is a bit ahead of his time. But he is super enthusiastic about what he is doing. And he got some big wheels in the travel industry interested too.

"Here is what is gonna happen," Hogarth say to about a dozen of us at Hobbema Pool Hall one afternoon. "The people who sell holidays are the travel agents – so I talked the Department of Tourism into sponsoring a tour of this reserve, not for tourists but for travel agents. The World Travel Convention is in Edmonton, and next week we going to bus down a hundred Italian travel agents to see the reserve. If they like the idea there could be thousands of tourists here next summer and then we can expand to other reserves all across Canada and the USA."

"Why would we want tourists?" ask Frank.

"One word," says Hogarth, and he smile even wider than he usually does. "Money."

"*I* can relate to that," grin Frank.

"There is going to be two classes of tour," Hogarth go on. "The regular tourists stay in the TraveLodge in Wetaskiwin or if they're real rich in the Chateau Lacombe in Edmonton, and we bus them down to the reserve to look around. The more adventurous ones, they get to stay with an Indian family, sleep in your house, eat with you..."

"I hear Italians like spaghetti," says Frank. "They'll be happy to find out Kraft Dinner is the national dish on Indian Reserves."

"No. No. You got it all wrong. Any place where we're gonna house a tourist will get special food allotments. You'll serve venison steak for breakfast, maybe badger stew for lunch, and roast moose for supper. We'll get the places cleaned up too, send down a maid service from Wetaskiwin, and we'll loan you dishes and bedding..."

"In other words the tourists get to see what you want them to see?" I say.

"Of course. That's the way it is all over the world. You guys have hardly been anywhere but tourists get the idea everywhere they go that the people are happy, eat good, and dance folk dances every day. And that's what they want to think. Look, I'm in show business. Fencepost, you're an actor, a liar, a thief, you understand that."

"Thanks for the good words," says Frank. "I understand what you're doing. What I don't get is why these foreigners want to come to see us anyway. I mean nobody in Canada want to come to our reserve. Even *we* don't like living here very much."

"It's the romance of the unknown," say Hogarth, bite the end off a flashlight-sized cigar. "Silas, you read a lot. There must be some places you'd like to visit."

"I'd like to see these here pygmies in Africa," I say.

"You figure the pygmies would like to see you?"

"Probably not."

"Right. They don't think they're unique. They hunt and fish and just try to survive. But we think they're special, and if you had a lot of money you'd pay to go look at them and their villages, taste what they eat, see them dance."

"I hear you," I say.

"Italians, Germans, most Europeans think you're unique. They've read bad books about Indians, seen American movies, looked at romantic pictures of Indian life. They'll pay good money to *experience* Indians first hand. And I'm here to cash in on their desires and see that you guys cash in too. Now Silas, if you went all the way to Africa to see a pygmy village, you'd be disappointed as hell if you found them wearing T-shirts advertising rock-and-roll singers, watching TV, and eating fast food, wouldn't you?"

"We might be able to cooperate a little," I say.

Bedelia Coyote, who we sometimes call the Queen of the Causes, because she is in favor of so many things, get all excited about the tourists coming.

"The way to retain our culture is to share it," she say. "We demonstrate our crafts, our dances, our foods, our music, and by doing so for the public we keep the customs alive and convince young people to carry on our traditions."

Sometimes I worry about Bedelia. She is so political and socially conscious she getting to sound like a politician. I don't know how wide the line is she walking on but I'm afraid she is going to fall over and by trying to be the *best* of us, she going to become the *worst* of *them*.

First thing she does is sweet talk Mad Etta into being a tourist attraction.

"Just like Mt. Eisenhower," says Frank.

"Only larger," I say, looking around to be sure Etta is not within earshot.

"Etta will take visitors to the woods, show them how to gather roots, leaves, herbs. Then she'll show how to cook with herbs and how to make simple medicines," Bedelia say to Hogarth. We have brought him to Etta's cabin.

"Etta knows the recipe for Kentucky Fried Chicken," says Frank. "She can name all 11 herbs and spices."

I read somewhere that Kentucky Fried Chicken made with black pepper, salt, and one other thing that I can't pronounce. So I guess the Colonel did have a secret recipe after all.

"Excuse me," say Hogarth staring right past Etta as if she don't exist. "Listen, Silas, I know you understand, so maybe you can explain things to the old woman over there and what's-her-name." He don't have any idea how lucky he is to have Bedelia on his side. "It's a matter of concept, see. I mean, I'm not questioning her ability. I'm sure she's good and all that, but she doesn't look like a medicine man. I mean, first of all we need a *man*, a handsome old man who *looks* wise, and knows how to wear buckskins and elk-tooth jewelry.

"You know what I mean, man. He can babble away in Cree and you or Frank or me, we can translate anything we feel like. You tell the old woman to go back to brewing her herb tea, I'm sure she'll understand."

Etta rumble deep within herself like the beginning of a rock slide.

"Oh, she'll understand alright," I say.

"Good," say Hogarth, dismissing the idea of Etta. "Now, that old blind man you showed me sitting on the porch of the General Store, Louis, wasn't it? He'd make a great medicine man. We'll dress him up and, he just has to sit and look wise. Blind draws a lot of sympathy, you know what I mean?"

"Do I get to keep the clothes?" is the first question Louis Coyote ask when I tell him what Hogarth Running Eagle wants to do.

I take it on myself to tell him, "Sure."

"Boots, too?"

"You only got one leg, Louis."

"Boots," Louis insist. "Hand-tooled, have eagles and arrows and maybe some Cree writing on them. Eustace Sixkiller made a pair like that while he was in prison. I've always wanted them."

It take two meetings between Hogarth and me before he agree to boots. "As long as they're Indian boots," he say, "maybe we can get the bootmaker to demonstrate his craft?"

I make it clear I ain't approaching Eustace Sixkiller. He is as mean a dude as I've ever known. Did time for manslaughter, and he carry an eight-inch awl, called a Saskatchewan toothpick, in each boot. He use them like tattoo needles, make somebody he don't like bleed like a fresh-water spring.

"Okay, forget the bootmaker," say Hogarth. He then

spend an extra hour explain just what he want from us. "I want you to think Indian," he tell us.

"I belong to a Back to the Land group," say Bedelia. "It led by an old Chief, a man who know all the old ways. They live 80 miles back in the hills, hunt and fish for food, live in tepees, make their own clothes. You could show them off..."

"No. We don't want anything that primitive. Those people would be poor, maybe smell bad. What we want is a...a happy medium."

One thing we find is Hogarth want that happy medium to happen *now*. He should know that us Indians like to think things over for quite a while before we actually take any action.

The next time Hogarth come to the reserve he ain't near so friendly. In fact he is all business. Guess he has developed what Mr. Nichols call a *sense of urgency*, which Mr. Nichols say most of us Indians was born without, and a good thing too.

"You look like hippies," Hogarth yell at us, when he find us lounging in the sun in front of Ben Stonebreaker's Hobbema General Store. "Jesus, look at you!" he holler at Frank, who wearing a cape he cut from some curtains he find in somebody's garbage, and a white glove with the fingers cut off. "What are you, the wagonburner's Michael Jackson? I want INDIANS! You're all dressed like cowboys, for chrissakes. I want braids, wampum, spears, bows and arrows, loincloths, buckskin, campfires, pinto ponies, hides nailed to the outside walls of your cabins, tepees, travois, trick riding. You guys never seen any Western movies? Listen," and he bang the flat of his hand against his forehead, "I got 100 ignorant Wop travel agents to impress.

"Remember what we were talking about the other day? I

want to see Old Time Indians...REAL INDIANS..."

"Real Indians don't eat egg McMuffins," says Frank.

"Real Indians roll their own," say Eathen Firstrider, who able to build a cigarette with one hand while ride on a saddle horse.

"Real Indians don't wear designer jeans," says Connie Bigcharles.

"Real Indians don't stuff saskatoon berries up their noses..."

"Enough, enough," say Hogarth Running Eagle, and his car wheels spin out gravel as he drive away mad. I think Mr. Nichols know what he talking about when it come to that *sense of urgency*.

In spite of the way Hogarth treated Mad Etta, everything would of been okay if only he hadn't welshed on the money he promised us.

I wasn't surprised. One day I asked Mr. Nichols to explain that word "entrepreneur."

"It's just a fancy way of saying organizer," say Mr. Nichols, "but it has a mainly negative connotation or meaning in our society. Usually an entrepreneur is a hustler who has no money, often calls his business 'Something Enterprises Ltd' and you'd better get your money up front when you're dealing with one, and count the fillings in your teeth and the number of fingers on each hand after he's left."

Hogarth keep postponing the money we been promised for a show. At least he buy Louis Coyote that fancy pair of boots. When he do he pay Eustace Sixkiller cash money, and treat him with respect. Eustace got dark blue tattoos on all his arms and shoulders.

We have a hard time getting Louis to wear his new boots. "I appreciate things with my fingers," he says, his blind eyes look into the distance. His old, brown fingers feel the soft leather and tooled designs, and he hold the leather to his nose and appreciate it that way too.

Hogarth rehearse Louis for his part, again and again.

"Impart them some Indian wisdom," say Hogarth.

Louis push his mirrored glasses down on his nose, so me and a few other people can glimpse his milky eyes.

"I'm only wearing one spur," he say slowly and with dignity. Then he pause a long time. "Do you want to know how a blind man can tell he is only wearing one spur?"

"Yes," several of us say, pretending we is Italian tourists.

Louis bang the heel of the boot with the spur on the floor. The spur clank real loud. Then he bang the boot without the spur.

"My ears tell me," he say, and smile behind his glasses. "They also tell me which boot it is on."

We all go, "Ooooh," and, "Aaaah."

"Maybe if we put a little curl in his hair," say Hogarth. "There's such a thing as looking too Indian."

My guess is we going to have to change most of the entertainment part of the program we lined up. At least the parts that ain't very Indian, like Matthias Two Young Men, who is all set to sing "Arrivederci Roma." Matthias fancy himself another Julio Iglesias looking for a place to happen, so he rented a tuxedo with a frilly blue shirt from Bozniak's Formal Rentals and Party Supplies in Edmonton, oiled his hair, greased his smile, and actually put wax on his teeth, after he brushed them for about two hours.

The two big doubledecker charter buses with tinted glass windows and roofs, roll onto the reserve. It is a nice fall day, with a few yellow leaves still clinging to the trees, and a woodsmoke smell in the air.

We have a troupe of chicken dancers going full tilt as the

travel agents step off the buses. My sister Delores whirr like a trail bike as she point her feather bustle at the visitors and dance up a storm.

Louis Coyote sit on a stump in his front yard.

"Able to predict the weather accurately, year after year," Hogarth tell the travel agents. Hogarth could pass for a Member of Parliament; he wear an expensive royal-blue suit, and had his hair styled special, "long enough to let them know I'm Indian, but conservative enough to let them know I'm a reliable businessman," is how he describe it. Speaking of Members of Parliament, Chief Tom turned up all set to deliver a half-hour welcome speech, but the drums for the chicken dancers drown him out. Now he standing on the sidelines looking ugly, thinking I bet of going back to Wetaskiwin and feeling sorry for himself.

Louis make his weather predictions. Do some rigmarole about heavy fur growing on the north side of gophers. We all laugh behind our hands, but the travel agents eat it up. He do his bit about the spur. But then there is a long silence.

"Is that all?" say Hogarth in a stage whisper.

Chief Tom take a deep breath and I can see he getting ready to fill in the gap.

"What do you expect from an old man?" says Louis. "I have 19 children," he say to the travel agents. They all scribble notes on their clipboards.

"Eighteen," say Mrs. Blind Louis, who been standing quiet by the cabin door.

"Do not most of those who ride on the range wear two spurs, if you please?" ask a travel agent in broken English; he is short and round and covered all over in a blue-striped suit.

"Ah," sigh Louis, "if one side of the horse runs can the other be far behind?"

"Now that's what I'm paying him for," say Hogarth with

great satisfaction.

"Speaking of money," I say.

"Not now," say Hogarth into my ear. "You'll get paid if I make a deal with the travel agents, and when and if I feel like it."

"I was only asking," I say. He don't even see me shake my head at somebody on the far edge of the crowd.

Hogarth parade the travel agents over to Blue Quills Hall, where he's sweet talked the Blue Quills Ladies Auxiliary into serving fried rabbit, bannock, and saskatoon pie; he has promised them they'll get paid later.

The lunch go off without a hitch, though there is about 40 pieces of fried rabbit left over because Mad Etta didn't show up for free food like she usually do. Hogarth is just about to walk the agents from Blue Quills Hall over to where Frank Fencepost, David One-wound, Eathen and Rufus Firstrider, and a few other guys is painted up to look like a raiding party, when there is a great growl like a semitrailer starting up, and the side door to Blue Quills Hall push open with a crash. That door open *out*, so you know how hard it been pushed. The long black arm of a bear hold that torn screen door in the air, then toss it halfway across the hall. The bear growl again and force most of itself through the door.

The travel agents scream, and many of them shout, "Orso," which I don't need an interpreter to tell me mean *bear* in Italian.

They bang open the double door at the front of the hall and scramble across the gravel and into their big buses, all the time pushing and shoving and yelling. There is a trail of high-heeled shoes, notepads, pens, hats, sunglasses and souvenirs, strewn all across the parking lot, look like flowers been scattered.

Chief Tom's big, black Lincoln Continental is already

164

100 yards down the road and picking up speed.

"It's only a joke. It's only a joke," Hogarth keep repeating as the bus motors start.

The bear ain't come out of the hall. It is helping itself to the leftover rabbit.

Hogarth turn to me with a look of panic on his face. "How the hell do you say *joke* in Italian?"

"Real Indians don't speak Italian," I tell him.

THE FOG

My littlest sister Delores come running through the door-way of our cabin puffing. "Silas, Silas, there's a phone call for you down at the store."

I can tell she has run all the way; her braids are unravelled, her cheeks pink, and she smell of the outdoors. The phone is a half mile down the hill at Ben Stonebreaker's Hobbema General Store. As we walk down, I hold onto Delores' hand, and every once in a while we skip a step or two, Delores all the time talking a mile a minute. "Hurry up!" she say, pulling on my arm. But I ain't expecting a phone call so anybody who needs to talk to me can wait until I get there.

The phone is nailed to one of the back walls of the store. It made of varnished wood, is about a yard tall, and I bet is older than I am. I'm tall enough to talk into the mouth-piece, while most everybody else have to stand on their tiptoes, yell up as if they talking to someone at the top of a hill.

"Mr. Ermineskin," say a man's deep voice, the kind that set plates to rattling on the table if he was at your house. "My name is J. Michael Kirkpatrick and I'm Bureau Chief for Best North American News Service. I've read your books and I'm very impressed. Very impressed."

That means he's going to ask me to do some work for him:

interview somebody, write a column or something. The point I have to establish quick is, is he going to pay me, and if so, how much. Lots of people figure they can pay Indians with colored beads like in the old days; others figure that just because I'm an Indian I should be willing to work cheap.

I listen to what Mr. Kirkpatrick have to say, and I go "Ummmmm," and "Uh-huh," at the proper points so he won't figure the phone has gone dead.

"As you are probably aware, the Pope is on a cross-country tour of Canada. One of his stops will be at Fort Simpson in the Northwest Territories, where he will meet with several thousand native people. We would like you to cover that event as a representative of Best North American News Service, and to write about it from a native point of view, so to speak."

"How much?" I ask. I've learned from sad experience not to be shy about taking money. Editors have kept me on the phone for an hour, or I've sat in a carpeted office listening to a long explanation of an assignment, only to find out they expect to pay me twenty dollars or less for the job.

Mr. Kirkpatrick name a figure. I ask for double. He say no way. I say goodbye. He raise his price $250. I say okay.

It is while he is telling me that I going to get to ride on a chartered airplane that I get my idea.

"How would you like to not have to pay me at all?" I say.

"What's the deal?"

"Well, if you were to send two of my friends along with me, we'd settle for expenses. Medicine lady of our tribe was saying just last night how she'd like to meet the Pope. And I got a close friend I want to bring with me."

"Girlfriend, eh?" say Mr. Kirkpatrick.

"No," I say. "It's a man."

"Oh, well, I suppose it's okay." He sound kind of embarrassed. "Somehow I never thought of you Indians being *that way*. But I suppose you *are* a writer."

Boy, when I tell Mad Etta what I arranged she get as excited as I ever seen her.

"I want to have a talk with this Pope guy," she say. "You know him and me ain't so different. People believe in what he got to hand out – I can't figure out why – but in the long run it don't matter. For me, having people believe in my cures is about 90% of the battle. Maybe I can make a trade with this Mr. Pope. I seen him on the TV the other day and I can tell by the way he holds himself that he still got pains from the time he got shot. I'll take him some cowslip roots to boil up; maybe I'll even boil it for him. If he drinks the tea his pain will go away."

"Yeah, but what can he do for you?"

"I'm not real sure. But he's a nice man. And, if you stop to think about it, he believes in the old ways, just like us. Maybe I can learn from him something about *influence*. I mean we got over 4,000 people, but only about a hundred or so believe in me. I could use the secret of attracting more followers."

Frank's biggest wish is to get Pope John Paul to bless his lottery tickets. "I'll donate 10% of my winnings to his church. And I'd really like to have him get me a part in that *Knight Rider* TV show. I want to drive that superpowered car that talks like a person."

"Those ain't the kinds of miracles the Pope usually get asked for," I say.

"Right. He must get tired of being asked to cure rheumatism and back aches. I figure he'll pay attention to an unusual request."

"But you don't believe."

"Not yet. I will as soon as that car from *Knight Rider* pull on to the reserve and say, 'Come here, Frank Fencepost.

I been dying to have you drive me.'"

Though it is the fall season here in Alberta, with the days warm and the trees still covered with pumpkin-colored leaves, we take parkas and sleeping bags with us. We been to the Arctic once, Frank and me, and it was below zero there, in real temperature, even in the summer.

We sit Etta on her tree-trunk chair in the back of Louis Coyote's pickup truck and drive to the little airport in the middle of Edmonton. Like they promised, Best North American News Service have an airplane waiting. It is small, hold four passsengers and a pilot, but it is new. I promised myself I'd never fly in a small plane again after I went to Pandemonium Bay in a plane with doors that wouldn't close and windows where the snow blew right in, and an engine about as powerful as a sick Skidoo. But this is another time.

The pilot wear a uniform just like he was in the air force.

"Take us to see the Pope, General," Frank say, salute the pilot. "You got champagne and movies on this here flight?"

"But the pilot pay about as much attention to Frank as if he was a fly buzzing around his head; what he *is* staring at is Mad Etta.

"It's alright," I tell him. "She's a medicine lady; you'll never crash with her aboard."

Etta is decked out in a new deerskin dress. "Deer population will be down for years to come," is what Frank said when he first seen it. The dress got about 10 pounds of porcupine quills on it, including a purple circle on Etta's front the size of a garbage can lid.

"Getting her aboard is what I'm worried about," says the pilot. "That door don't expand."

He's right. The little steps up to the door are like toys, and even ordinary people have to duck and turn to get inside.

"Hey, when I want to do something I get it done," say

Etta. "Silas, you go inside and pull; Frank, you push."

Moving Etta is kind of like moving furniture. I seen guys get sofas and deepfreezes up twisting stairs and through doors smaller than the things they were moving.

Etta give the directions and we do the work. A couple of times I figure Etta going to get stuck permanent. Then it look like the door-frame gonna split on us, or else Etta is. I think finally Etta just concentrate and shrink herself about four inches all around, for she pop through the door like she been greased.

During the flight Etta sit on one side of the plane, while me, Frank, and the pilot, and all our luggage sit on the other.

"The News Service has a bigger plane waiting in Yellow-knife to take you on to Fort Simpson," the pilot tell us.

It is in Yellowknife where the real trouble start. There is hundreds and hundreds of reporters in the tiny airport, waiting to get any kind of aircraft to fly them to the even tinier airport in Fort Simpson. There's also several TV people from Best North American News Service, who is determined to get to Fort Simpson.

"Your friends are gonna have to stay behind," say a camera-man, who is chewing on a cigar, look like Charles Bronson when he been without sleep for two days.

"No way," I say. "I'm working for nothing so my friends can go along."

"Look, no one ever thought of the shortage of transporta-tion. Everything's been cleared with J. Michael Kirkpatrick back in Toronto. You get paid your full fee plus a $500 bonus. Your friends get a hotel room here in Yellowknife and their meals until you get back from Fort Simpson. They're lucky not to be going. It's gonna be a madhouse there."

It don't look like I have no choice. Boy, I sure hate to

explain the change to Etta. When she hear what I have to say she rumble deep inside like bad plumbing.

"When Etta get mad she usually get even," I tell the Best North American people. But not knowing Etta, they ain't impressed.

There is more trouble when I get on the plane. Frank has found a seat for himself next to a lady.

"I'm editor of this here Indian newspaper called *The Moccasin Telegraph*," he is telling her as I come down the aisle. I notice he is already touching her body. "Ah, here's my assistant now. His name is Silas Gopher; he's sort of my gofer," and Frank laugh loud and hearty. He also have a jack-handle laid across his lap and when somebody from the airline tell him to move, he suggest he will do a certain amount of damage to anybody who try to take his seat from him. The pilot and his assistant have a quick meeting and decide to leave Frank where he is; instead they let the cameraman sit in the aisle. If only Frank had thought to bring Etta with him.

You know how, when a special visitor is coming you clean up your house. You do things you would never ordinarily do, like wash in corners, clean things and places a visitor would never look. Well, that is the way it is with the whole town of Fort Simpson. The town is not very big to start with, only a thousand people they tell us. Fort Simpson is located where the Laird and Mackenzie Rivers meet, it is the trading place for all the native peoples for hundreds of miles. It seem to me everyone of them people must have come to Fort Simpson to see the Pope. Boy, I really have never seen so many Indians in one place at one time.

"Where's our hotel?" is the first question Frank ask after we hit the ground.

"Ha," says the cameraman. "See that row of tents down along the riverbank. That's where we stay. There's only one small hotel in town and it's been booked up forever. Shouldn't be any problem for you guys though. Indians are used to living outdoors."

"*Some* Indians," I say.

I should have asked more questions before I took this job. I mean knowing about the outdoors don't come naturally to Indians. Me and Frank aren't campers or hunters or trackers. We like hotel rooms, Kentucky Fried Chicken, video games, riding in taxis, and electric guitars. But it look like we going to have to do without those things for a few days. What *is* here is like a disorganized carnival with no main event.

It is Government money that keep Fort Simpson in business, so it is Government people who organize for the Pope's visit. People who work full time for the Government is there 'cause they ain't competent enough to work anywheres else. All around town they have really spent a lot of money to show how smart they *ain't*.

To start with some bureaucrat must have ordered a thousand gallons of whitewash. All the sad buildings in this little town, what haven't even a memory of a coat of paint, have been sloshed with whitewash. Coming down on the airplane, these buildings looked like extra big, white birds scattered across the barren land.

These same Government people also imported rolls and rolls of fake grass. It is fall and what little grass there is is brown. The town is mostly rock and mud. Now, in all kinds of unlikely places is little blazes of green.

"What harm do you suppose it would do the Pope to see the land the way it really is?" ask Frank.

"If he's got a direct connection to God, then he'll know what he's seeing is phony and it won't matter," I say.

Every rock within eyesight of Fort Simpson also been whitewashed.

"Looks like Limestone City," says a reporter.

"I wonder if they bath the people as they come into town, wouldn't want the Pope to smell anything bad," says someone else.

"Didn't you hear?" says a CBC cameralady, "night before the visit they're gonna whitewash us. We'll all glow like foxfire the day of the big visit."

"I wonder what we're gonna do to kill time," I say. It is only Saturday. The Pope ain't due until Tuesday. I been at events where the reporters interview each other they get so desperate for news.

All along the riverbank for as far as we can see is square little pup tents in a long row.

"That's the Press Area," somebody tells us. "Better grab yourself a tent before they're all gone."

I'm sure glad we brought heavy clothes. There are little propane heaters and portable cookstoves in the tents, but it easy to see the first arrivals been having trouble with them, 'cause about every tenth tent been burned down.

Frank and that lady TV producer he met on the plane have decided to share a tent. That evening Frank win a fair amount of money in a card game until somebody point out which side of the deck he's dealing from.

"Indians always deal from the bottom of the deck," Frank say in a serious voice, acting as if he is the one been offended. He at least bluff his way out of any broken bones, though after that no one will play cards with him anymore.

Just as I'm afraid of, since I appear to be the only Indian reporter in town, I get interviewed by other reporters for radio, TV and newspapers. They are all disappointed that I'm not excited about being here. "I'm sure this Pope is a nice man, but as I see it the Church and smallpox have done about equal damage to the Indian people over the years," I tell them. I don't think they ever broadcast or print that. Nobody want to say anything negative about anything, especially the Pope.

The natives, or the *Dene*, as the Indians call themselves, have got things pretty well organized in spite of having the Government looking over their shoulders.

"There are over 8,000 visitors here," a Cree chief from near Yellowknife tell us. Later, I heard there was only 4,000 people all told. When that guy from the news service called me he said to expect 40,000. I notice that a lot of people who have come are really old. They come off the roads in pickup trucks as beat up as the one we drive at home, all dusty, rusty and coughing; they come down the rivers in all kinds of boats powered by stuttering outboards.

Out on the flats is a tent city, not the new canvas of the press tents, but canvas stitched and repaired and patched, sun faded to the color of the hills in late fall. Lived-in tents with smoke blackening around the tops where north winds pushed smoke down against the canvas. That field of tents look exactly like pictures and paintings of old time Indian settlements I've seen at the Glenbow Museum in Calgary.

The women have set up racks of spruce logs for the curing of moose meat, deer, caribou, whitefish and speckled trout.

In the huge tepee that been built to honor the Pope, drums been throbbing day and night, and dancers dance old-time circle dances. A few, but not many of the dancers are in costume. This is real dancing by men in denim and deerskins, women in long skirts and saggy sweaters – real people, not people dressed in plastic beads and feathers made in Korea who practise their dancing on a government grant.

The people here call the Pope *Yahtitah*; it mean priest-father, as near as I can translate.

Lots of the reporters and many of the Indians have transistor radios, listen to what happen in the outside world.

"He's taking off from Edmonton Airport any minute now," someone report on Tuesday morning, his hand holding the tiny black radio close to his ear. "He'll be here right on schedule."

Then about 10 minutes later, "Take-off's been delayed for 15 minutes."

The circle dancing continues. Smoke the same color of the sky drift in the cool, damp air of morning.

"His plane's developed engine trouble," someone say. "Departure from Edmonton is delayed by 45 minutes."

Nobody's worried yet. But I imagine I can hear Etta rumbling in her room in that hotel in Yellowknife. If she got anything to cook on I bet she boiling up mysterious stuff.

After the delay stretch to over two hours people start to get nervous.

"He's gonna change planes," a reporter cry.

Everyone cheer and clap. The drums in the compound get louder, like they applauding too.

"They're switching to a back-up plane; take-off's in 20 minutes."

Frank busy taking bets on the Pope's arrival time. He sit behind a table, in front of a sign he printed himself read, Frank Bank. He offers to bet money that the Pope don't arrive at all, give 2-1 odds. Indians take him up on that and the pile of money in front of him grow.

"He's takin' off!" and a cheer rise over the settlement like slow thunder. First time I ever hear a whole town make, as Pastor Orkin back home would say, "a joyful noise."

The weather been perfect Indian Summer ever since we arrived. That morning it was foggy first thing, but, as it supposed to do, the sun burn that fog off, and it was clear with a high sky when the take-off finally announced.

Over the next few hours, as the Pope fly through the air toward us, the clouds roll in, filmy and white as smoke tendrils at first, then it is like the sky develop a low roof, won't let the campfire smoke out. Fog all of a sudden rise off the river, twist around our ankles like a cat rubbing. For a while the sun look like a red balloon, then get dull as an orange, fade to the color of a grapefruit, disappear altogether.

The drum slow down as if people's hearts beating slower.

"He's due in five minutes," someone shout. The drums stop and those thousands and thousands of people stare up into the fog. It is so thick I have to strain my eyes to see the top of that 55-foot tepee out on the flats. If I get more than a hundred yards away it look like a shadow of a tepee, the real thing hid from me by a gray blanket.

The long drone of an airplane fill the air, but it is very high and going right past us, not landing.

"Too foggy," call the people with the radios attached to their ears. "Pilot gonna try again."

A whisper pass through the crowd like a shiver. The word "pray" is whispered from a few thousand mouths. People all around me bow their heads and move their lips silently. The fog is cold and a mean breeze cut through my clothes like a razor blade.

The plane make another pass over us.

The fog doesn't budge an inch.

There is a kind of keening sound rise from the enclosure of tents. I feel sorry for the old people who come hundreds of miles down river or cross-country to see this man. I'm sorry too that these people have abandoned their own religion out of fear, for something the white man force on them. If it wasn't for guns there wouldn't be but a handful of Indian Christians.

"There's only enough fuel for one more pass," someone say.

"If there was anything to their religion don't you figure their god could move aside a few clouds?" I say to no one in particular, though I got Mad Etta in mind.

The plane make its final pass and buzz away until it is less than a mosquito sound. People are actually weeping.

"We just wanted him to touch us," say an old woman in a sky-blue parka that glazed with dirt.

"They say he's gonna land in Yellowknife instead. He might come here tomorrow if it's clear."

People who come from the Yellowknife area groan with disbelief.

"Why Yellowknife? It's not on his schedule."

"They say the Pope feel a call to stop at Yellowknife and deliver a message."

At the news that he may come to Fort Simpson tomorrow, some people give a small cheer. The drums start up again and people go back to their dancing and hoping.

"That bit about him coming tomorrow is a lie," say a producer from Best North American News Service. "They're gonna wait until late tonight to announce he's not coming. Some bureaucrat in Yellowknife is afraid of a riot."

Frank have to wait hours and hours to collect his bets. But now, people who like lost causes are putting down money that the Pope will show. It is kind of like by betting on the Pope they are showing off their faith.

"I was hoping I'd feel something," a girl about my age say to me, just after she place a five dollar bet. "The old people believed he could change things. I want to believe like them, but I just don't know..." and her voice fade away.

Somebody sum it up good when they say, "Same as the church always do; they promise a whole lot and deliver nothing."

Nobody seems very mad, except the press people, who put in four ugly, cold days and now have nothing to write about. Some of them scared up a legend or two, about a church that was burned down, or that a great leader would die at a place where two rivers meet. And somebody else get an old medicine man to say the animals been behaving strangely for the last few days.

But the Chief of the Slaveys state the believers' attitude the next morning when he say, "The *Dene* understand weather," and after long pause, "better than most."

During the Pope's unexpected stop in Yellowknife he record a radio message for all the people in Fort Simpson. He speak strong words about Native Rights and independence. The Yellowknife TV station was there, and early next morning their tape run on the CBC and we get to see it in Fort Simpson.

"There ain't nowhere in the world you can escape from the CBC," is what Frank says, and I guess it is true.

Just like the producer say, at 11:00 p.m. that night they announce that the Pope's visit to Fort Simpson is cancelled forever. The Pope will fly to Ottawa as planned. "Serious consideration was given to a Fort Simpson visit," they say, "but it would have ruined the Ottawa program."

"We all know they wouldn't want to ruin anything for the fat cats in Ottawa," laugh one of the reporters. "Even the Pope can't pass up the bureaucrats. I wonder how many of them came a thousand miles in a canoe down dangerous rivers to see him?"

The words of the cancellation announcement ain't cold in the air before the fog lift like it was being vacuumed, in ten minutes a butter-yellow moon and stars like tinsel light up the night.

The big surprise on the TV show from Yellowknife is that

on the balcony of the hotel, where the Pope speak to about 20 microphones, right beside him, the purple circle on the front of her dress pulsing like a strobe light, was Mad Etta. Etta smiling like she know more secrets than the Pope, and, as he wave to his friends, she wave to hers.

INDIAN JOE

I never forget the Christmas my sister Illianna got Indian Joe as a present. Pa had left us the year before and Delores was just a baby. I remember Delores peering over Ma's shoulder as we walk down the hill from our cabin to Blue Quills Hall, where the Christmas party was.

There was a big, tall Christmas tree inside Blue Quills Hall. The place smell smokey because the stove backed up. Each of us kids was gived a candy cane and a glass of lemonade. Everyone sat around with their coats on acting shy.

Finally Santa Claus showed up. All but the littlest kids could tell it was Sven Sonnegard, a mechanic at the Husky Service Station on the highway. He still got his greasy, steel-toed work boots on below his Santa Claus suit.

There were galvanized garbage cans on the stage, each covered in green and red paper, each got a sheet of black construction paper taped to it, with BOY or GIRL and different age groups written on in chalk.

We got in a long line and when a kid got to the top of the stairs to the stage, he would sneak across toward Santa Claus, head down. If Sven Sonnegard could get the kid to tell its age, he'd reach in the right barrel for a present. If the kid wouldn't

180

tell, Sven would guess; sometimes he'd even have to guess if it was a boy or girl. One garbage can say BABY, others 1-3, 4-6, 7-9, and so on.

My friend Frank Fencepost notice the presents get bigger as the kids get older. When it's our turn, Frank he walk right up to Santa Claus and say, "Hi, Sven, I'd like to buy a quart of home-brew."

"Shut up, Kid," Sven say out of the side of his mouth, but he also have a hard time keep from laughing. We all know Sven make his living bootlegging, mainly to Indians.

"How old are you?" Sven say to Frank.

We are supposed to be in the 7-9 group.

"Fifteen," say Frank, push out his skinny chest, look Sven right in the eye.

"You ain't a day over eight," say Sven-Santa Claus.

"He's small for his age," I say.

"That's right, he's small for eight."

"I seen Constable Greer down by the door," said Frank. "How many cases of home-brew you think he'd find in your truck if he looked?"

Sven reach in the BOY 13-15 barrel, pull out a big package.

"My twin brother is at home sick," say Frank.

Santa Claus reach out another package, a basketball, and he nearly knock Frank over he push it into his arms so hard.

"My brother's brother couldn't be here neither."

Sven load another present into Frank's arms.

The line-up behind us getting restless.

"And my cousin..."

"Move along," said Santa. "What a good boy you've been," and push Frank so he skid clear across the stage.

"How old are you, Sport?" he said to me.

"Thirteen," I said, swallowing hard.

"Sure you are." He reach in the BOY 7-9 barrel and give

me a package turn out to be a peg-board game got half the wooden nubbins missing.

It was at this party Illianna was gived Indian Joe. Joe was a mechanical Indian, run by batteries. He was six or eight inches tall, sit on his haunches in front of a drum, with little drumsticks raised up ready to play. In Joe's lower back was a switch, and when it pressed down he play. H-H-H-Rap, Tap-Tap, go the drum. The toys we was given was all used, but Indian Joe was good as new and Illianna was real proud of him.

"He look something like Pa," Illianna say on the walk home. Her being older she remember Pa better than the rest of us. I never knew him to play the drum, or have black braids, or even a red shirt with green suspenders like Indian Joe.

After Illianna got her toy home she is kind of like a miser with her money when it come to sharing. She like him so much she take him to bed with her that first night.

All that happened about three years before Illianna go off to work in the city. By that time everybody but Illianna forgot about Indian Joe. No one even notice he is one of the things Illianna take to Calgary with her.

After she been in the city for a year or two my sister married herself to a white man name of Robert McGregor McVey. He is a big wheel in some company that loan out money. Me and my friends have caused McVey a certain amount of grief over the years. The first time I ever seen their new house, I discover that in their bedroom Illianna and Brother Bob have what's called a walk-in closet. On one of the shelves sat Indian Joe. He look smaller than I remember him, but except that one of the plastic feathers is gone from his war-bonnet, he is good as new. I remember thinking it is strange for Illianna to keep a toy like that, 'cause she been married for years and have her own little boy named Bobby.

Last week me and Frank went to Calgary for a day. We park the truck and start walking around.

"What should we do?" I ask Frank.

"Let's go in the lobby of a bank and watch people withdraw money from the machines," says Frank.

We watch the machines for a while.

Later, I seen a sign take me by surprise. In gold letters in the form of an arch, just like McDonald's, it say INTER-CONTINENTAL LOAN CO. LTD., Robert M. McVey, Division Manager.

"Look at that," I say to Frank. "You figure that's Brother Bob?"

"Let's go inside and see," he says.

We walk inside, and boy, the place is just like a bank. There is secretaries everywhere, dressed fancy as models. Quiet music is playing and typewriters tick. Everywhere there is machines look like a cross between typewriters and televisions.

"Good afternoon, may I help you?" a lady say. She is tall, with long blond hair, dressed in a brown, scratchy-looking suit, remind me of a doormat.

"I'd like to borrow 20 dollars," says Frank, give her a big smile. "I pay you back tomorrow for sure. I even leave my friend here. You can sell him if I don't come back."

The girl try hard to be polite.

"I'm afraid we only make industrial loans," she say.

"How about if you loan me twenty dollars personally?" say Frank, and he look at her real sad, lift up one finger point to his cheek. As he does a tear squeeze out of his eye, roll onto his cheek and stop there. Frank seen an Indian on TV do that, that Indian was sad about white men cutting down trees or something.

"How do you do that?" the girl says.

"Come real close and I show you."

The girl does, then turn to another girl and say, "Hey, Francine, come look at this."

"Maybe you've seen me on TV?" Frank saying.

Frank wipe the tears off his cheek, start the water flowing again.

"Excuse me," I say to a gray-haired lady, "is Mr. McVey in?"

"Whom should I say is calling?" she say, look right at me as if what she's asking ain't funny.

"Tell him his brother, Silas, is here."

She scowl, and I bet she is going to say something nasty to me when she remember that Brother Bob have an Indian wife. She push her face into a tiny smile and pick up a white telephone.

A few minutes later, Brother Bob, his cheeks all shiny, wearing a striped suit and vest, smell like he just bathed in shaving lotion, come out of a door labelled EXECUTIVE OFFICES.

He try to be friendly, but he is embarrassed to see me there. Bet he wishes he could dress me up in a suit like him and cut my hair.

"Why Silas," he say, "what a surprise!"

"I seen your name on the window."

Brother Bob stare around kind of nervous. Then his eyes light on Frank's back. Frank got five or six secretaries watching him cry. I notice he is also putting a stapler in his pocket.

"You *didn't* bring that Posthole with you?" Brother Bob yell.

"He's keepin' himself busy," I say. "You never even know he's here."

"Well, Silas, how would you like a tour of our business facilities?" he ask. "We've got straight state-of-the-art technology here. Everything is done by computer. I expect you'll be buying, or how is it you put it, creatively borrowing, a word processor to facilitate your writing procedures," and he give me a little chuckle.

"I facilitate my writing procedures with a felt pen and a Royal typewriter," I say. "I'm scared of these here computers."

"It's inevitable, Silas. People in the horse-and-buggy era were afraid of the horseless carriage. Now, even *you* drive a car..."

It get pretty noisy across the room where Frank and the secretaries gathered around a big copier. Brother Bob and me work our way over to them.

I guess Frank ain't ever seen a copying machine up close before. One of the secretaries show him how it work, and Frank put his hand down flat, push the button, and out come a piece of paper with a big, blue-black hand on it.

"Hey, I bet this here machine could copy food," cries Frank. "Silas," he yell, "run down to a restaurant and get a sandwich. I'll copy it enough times to feed the whole reserve." The secretaries all laugh. I notice a couple of them is already touching Frank.

"He doesn't really believe that, does he?" Brother Bob ask.

"Well..." I say. "Mad Etta teach him pretty strong medicine. If he was to copy a sandwich it just might come out real."

Brother Bob stare me up and down, but he don't have the nerve to call me a liar. He shoo all the secretaries back to their desks. Then he take both of us through a couple of metal doors, thick as the kind they have in warehouses, and into a room with no windows.

"This is our computer center," he say, wave one of his small, pink hands at the rows and rows of blinking machines.

The sounds in the room is quite a bit like an arcade, except all the humans is quiet.

"You keep the money inside those machines?" ask Frank.

"Oh, no," say Brother Bob, "no money, but all our records are in there. We can establish the status of any loan account in the nation in less than 10 seconds. Here, let me show you..." and he actually smile at us, looking kind of purplish under the artificial light.

As I look at Brother Bob, I wonder how Illianna feel about being married to a white man, and living in a white world. She seem to be happy, and says Bob and her have lots of friends. And she has her little boy Bobby. Still, no matter how I try, I can't "walk in her moccasins," as Mad Etta our medicine lady would say. I can't imagine not being with other Indians. It seem to me I'd get awful tired of always being on display, of answering dumb questions, of always being afraid I'd make a mistake.

Brother Bob poke away at the keys of a computer and a whole page of figures appear. "See," he says. I can tell by looking at Frank that he is just dying to touch one of these machines.

"Watch this," says Brother Bob. "This machine can speak too."

He push a button and the machine talk, sound like somebody under a foot of water with his nose plugged. But once I tune my ears to it, I can understand.

"Can you teach it to cuss?" ask Frank.

"I suppose I could, if I was so inclined," Brother Bob reply, but pretty coldly.

The steel door open and that gray-haired lady stick her head in. "Excuse me, Mr. McVey, but Zurich is on the line."

"I'll be right back," Brother Bob say to us, and trot away.

"Boy, this is just like a video arcade," yells Frank, move up to the word processor and poke a button or two. "Which one do I push to shoot down all those squiggley things?"

"I don't know if we should be touching these here machines," I say.

"Where's the coin slot?"

"Brother Bob own these machines. You don't have to pay to use them."

"Wow! Brother Bob is in heaven and I bet he don't even know it." Frank go from machine to machine, poke a button here and there.

"These ain't games..."

"But I bet they could be," and Frank whack a few more buttons.

"We better go," I say.

About that time, a red light, look like an ambulance flasher, high above the door, start flashing, and a bell, like a fire alarm, begin ringing.

"I think I got this one working," yells Frank.

It does look as if it's turning into a game. The red light flashes, the siren bongs, it is just like our favorite arcade in Wetaskiwin.

Just as Frank really starting to enjoy himself, Brother Bob come crashing through the door.

"Don't touch that machine anymore," he yells. "Our entire loan records are in there. If it goes down..."

"I'm gonna blow these little green suckers away," yells Frank, pound the buttons the way a Russian pianist I seen on TV pound his piano.

"That's enough, Frank," I'm surprised to hear myself saying. I move toward him, intending to pull him away from the machine. Sometimes it seem to me Frank don't think enough before he act.

"Don't hit that button..." scream Brother Bob. We both

dive for Frank. The machine look like it making fireworks and is about to explode.

I hit Frank like he was carrying a football and we both roll under a table, scatter a couple of wastebaskets across the room. Brother Bob shut off the machine, wipe his forehead, stare at us with his eyes bugging out.

I'm not sure if what I've done is good or bad.

"Another five seconds and our entire financial records would have been destroyed. Some of it could never be replaced."

I don't think Brother Bob realize that I was helping him. Maybe that's just as well. He march us both out of the building as if we was under arrest.

"We sure is sorry, Brother Bob," we say, but he don't even tell us goodbye.

Outside, Frank decide to wait the hour until closing time. He arranged to meet two or more of them secretaries. I decide to visit Illianna.

"We stopped in to see Brother Bob," I tell her. "He sure is busy, might be real late getting home tonight." By the way Illianna look at me I know she don't want to hear any details.

We have coffee at her kitchen table and I play with Bobby for a while, then say I'd better get going. I bet Brother Bob still ain't in a mood to be apologized to.

"I've got a present for Ma's birthday," Illianna say, "you can take it back with you." She get up and walk to her bedroom and I follow. She walk into the big closet take a package wrapped in flowered paper off a shelf. The package was sitting right beside Indian Joe.

"You still got old Indian Joe," I say, act kind of surprised.

"I got my doll, too," Illianna says, move aside a blanket and sure enough there is her one-eyed, bald doll, what at one

188

time had platinum-colored hair. Illianna touch Indian Joe on the top of the head. "We been through a lot," she says, smile sad at me.

Indian Joe still sit behind his drum, wear green felt suspenders down the front of his red shirt. His black braids hang straight as sticks. His arms hold up in awkward half-circles, the little wood drumsticks forever poised.

"He sure does bring back a lot of memories," I say. I flip the switch in Indian Joe's back. "H-H-H-Rap, Tap-Tap..." go Indian Joe, which surprise me a lot. I didn't think batteries lasted for so many years.

"H-H-H-Rap, Tap-Tap," he go again, and, as I switch him off, I look at Illianna 'cause I hear her make a funny sound. My eyes catch her face just in time to see it falling in on itself. The tears flood out of her big, brown eyes.

I hold out my arms to her. She takes one step forward and clasp onto me real hard.

"Is there anything I can do?" I ask.

"No, everything's alright, Silas. Really, everything's alright."

"I know," I tell her, though I'm not sure I do. I think I can guess what she's feeling. For Illianna I bet it's one of those times when the past seems so far away – so permanently lost. I've had the feeling myself, a terrible sense of loss, like someone important has died. But then there's the worse feeling of not being able to name the person who'd died. It's a little like looking at your own grave.

I just hold her for a while as she cries into my shoulder. I believe her when she says everything's alright.

Then I hear Bobby come pounding in the back door. "Mom! Mom!" he calls.

Illianna pulls back, take a deep breath, wipes her eyes with her hands, wipes her hands on her jeans.

"Coming, honey," she says, and squeezes my hand as she turns away and walks out of the room, leaving me and Indian Joe staring at each other.

ACKNOWLEDGMENTS

The following stories have previously appeared in magazines: TRUTH (*North Dakota Review, Alberta on Ice*), THE TRUCK (*Matrix*), TO LOOK AT THE QUEEN (*Wascana Review*), THE PRACTICAL EDUCATION OF CONSTABLE B.B. BOBOWSKI (*Event*), THE INDIAN NATION CULTURAL EXCHANGE PROGRAM (*Canadian Forum*), THE PERFORMANCE (*Descant*), THE BEAR WENT OVER THE MOUNTAIN (*Vancouver Magazine*), DANCING (*West Coast Review*), REAL INDIANS (*Waves*), THE FOG (*NeWest Review*), and INDIAN JOE (*Prism International*).

ABOUT THE AUTHOR

W.P. Kinsella was born in Edmonton, Alberta, and still lives in Western Canada. His first novel, *Shoeless Joe*, won the prestigious Houghton-Mifflin Award and the *Books In Canada* first novel award, and was recently made into the movie "Field of Dreams."

Kinsella is also the author of *The Iowa Baseball Confederacy* and several short story collections including *Red Wolf, Red Wolf* and *The Miss Hobbema Pageant.*